"I thought this goddess thing was some big secret.

"You make it sound so simple."

"It isn't, of course," Gloria says. "The relationship between a man and a woman is complicated. But men love to be touched in subtle, sensual ways."

"I don't have the foggiest idea what you're talking about." More than twenty years of diapers, teenage diatribes and dog hair on the sofa have beaten the sensuality right out of me. Or maybe I never had any in the first place.

Gloria smiles. "Every day for the last twenty years I've walked into the studio and become a femme fatale. I can turn it on and off like a faucet."

"So why didn't you turn it on for Matt Tucker? You'd have him on his knees proposing."

"It would feel too much like acting. In real life I don't want pretense. I want truth."

"My sentiments exactly," Tuck says from out of nowhere.

Gloria's mortified expression is definitely not acting.

PEGGY WEBB

Peggy Webb and her two chocolate Labs live in a hundred-year-old house not far from the farm where she grew up. "A farm is a wonderful place for dreaming," she says. "I used to sit in the hayloft and dream of being a writer." Now, with two grown children and more than forty-five romance novels to her credit, the former English teacher confesses she's still a hopeless romantic and loves to create the happy endings her readers love so well.

When she isn't writing, she can be found at her piano playing blues and jazz or in one of her gardens planting flowers. Still, Peggy's friends love to sit on her front porch inhaling jasmine from her Angel Garden and celebrating her victories—bestseller lists, writing awards, options for film *(Where Dolphins Go)* and audio books.

The Secret Goddess Code

Peggy Webb

THE SECRET GODDESS CODE

isbn-13:978-0-373-88146-8
isbn-10: 0-373-88146-0

This edition published by arrangement with Harlequin Books S.A.

TheNextNovel.com

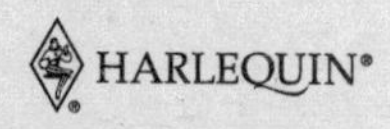

PRINTED IN U.S.A.

From the Author

Dear Reader,

My girlfriends and I claim to be goddesses, mostly of the kitchen. But is there more?

When I decided to explore the concept, I turned to my small-town roots—swings on the porch, pies in the oven, barbecue with the neighbors. What would happen if a real goddess landed in that environment?

I didn't have far to look for the perfect example.
My dear friend, actress Philece Sampler, provided an inspiration for Gloria. As Gloria bloomed on the pages of *The Secret Goddess Code*, I fell in love with her.

Of course, I fell in love with the sassy Jenny, too, as well as her daughter Angie and the outrageous Roberta. I present them with a dollop of magic and a generous sprinkling of stardust.

Thank you for writing to say how much you love my books. In appreciation, I'm doing a goddess contest. Details are on www.peggywebb.com.

Peggy

Johnie Sue and Jane, you are the rarest of friends—
my sounding board, my comforting shoulder, my giggling
pals, my fiercely loyal supporters, my memory, my strength
and my wings. Because of you, I'm still standing.
Did I mention that because of you (Jane), I can spell? And
because of you (Johnie Sue), I'm still sane? (Though some
would debate that. Only, not in front of you!)
This book is for the Big Three. Long may we reign!

Acknowledgments

I acknowledge dear friends Olivia Rupprecht, fellow writer who helped me find the heart of the story, and Philece Sampler, actress extraordinaire, whose unsinkable spirit inspired me. You rock, girlfriends!

CHAPTER 1

Where's the applause meter when you need it?
—Gloria

I have died and gone to Mooreville, Mississippi.

I knew things were bad when that peroxided, collagen-enhanced, nubile nymph Susan Star stole my role as the reigning TV goddess in *Love in the Fast Lane*, but I didn't know I'd be killed off for real and sent to the backside of nowhere. Good lord, just because a woman turns forty-five shouldn't mean she gets tossed out and consigned to life without long-stemmed roses and Godiva chocolates.

Trying to make sense of things, I close my eyes, but when I open them again I'm staring at the same wide expanse of cloudy sky slashed with a sign that says, Welcome to Mooreville. Plus, I have a lump on my head the size of California.

"Is anybody here?"

Expecting Saint Peter to answer, I ease up on my elbow and spot my powder-blue Ferrari Spyder. Or what remains of it. They don't let you take cars to the hereafter, no matter which way you go, so this means I'm not dead.

To some people that would come as a relief, but the mood I'm in, it just makes me mad.

It also makes me remember swerving to miss a cow, then clawing my way out of the airbag in an adrenaline-propelled panic, which explains why I'm in a ditch. My purse is upside down an arm's-length away so I scramble for my cell phone to dial 911. Alas, it's smashed into pieces against a rock. To add insult to injury, the big black clouds that have been hovering overhead let loose a flood that nearly washes me away.

Spotting a little convenience store down the road, I lurch upward intending to walk for help, but a pain rips through my ankle and throws me back down. They shoot horses with broken legs, don't they? It's not enough that my twenty-year career is over: I'm going to get shot or drown in a ditch.

When I left Hollywood and headed to my

childhood home in Jackson without even telling my agent, I expected headlines to read, Famous Soap-Opera Actress Disappears. I expected buzz in the biz would be that Gloria Hart had eloped to Paris or moved to a villa in the south of Italy or at the very least was last seen in a Piggly Wiggly filling a cart with Almond Joys and double-chocolate pudding.

Instead I've wrecked my car, maimed my cell phone and crippled myself, and there's not a single reporter around to turn this drama to my advantage. The situation calls for a major pity party.

I'm good at tears. Lord knows, I've had enough practice. After the writers put me in a fiery plane crash that killed off my fictional husband and swiped my fictional memory, I wept the Pacific Ocean on daytime TV and was flooded with sympathy letters from fans.

Now I try to work up a few tears, but all I can see is how ludicrous my situation is: done in by a cow and my crazy urge to drive Mississippi's back roads. I start laughing and can't stop.

Somebody get the net. I've gone completely crazy and sirens signal the men in white are coming to take me away.

"Are you all right?"

Oh, my lord. A drop-dead-handsome man in a fireman's uniform is talking to me. Either I bumped my head harder than I thought and am hallucinating, or Mooreville just started looking a whole lot better.

"That depends on how you describe all right."

I laugh again, probably teetering on the edge of hysteria, and the man who could be a *Playgirl* centerfold looks at me as if I'm from another planet. In a way, I guess I am. Hollywood is about as far from Mooreville as you can get. Beyond the man is an honest-to-goodness picket fence. And what looks like a black-and-white cow but just might be a big dog. The one that ran in front of my car and caused me to straddle a light pole.

And there's not a sidewalk in sight.

The hunk kneels over me and pops the blood-pressure cuff on while an older fireman and a paunchy state trooper scurry around my mutilated car.

"I'm Rick Miller, ma'am, and we're going to get you to the hospital over in Tupelo."

Now that makes me mad. My goodness, I'm not that badly injured.

The hunk, who is now checking me for broken bones, is wearing a wedding ring. Now maybe I *will* cry.

Not that I'm looking for a husband or anything remotely resembling one. But when a big chunk of your life gets ripped away and you don't have another person in this whole world to turn to, suddenly it feels as if you have nothing at all, as if you're teetering on the edge of a cliff in the middle of a deserted jungle screaming for a net, and there's not even a slim chance anybody will hear. It's times like this that make me long to have a good man who will hold me close and say "Everything is going to be all right."

"Listen, Rick, thanks for your offer. I'm a little rattled. It's not every day I run into a light pole. I don't know what I'm going to do about my poor car."

"I'll call Tuck's Tow Service. Jackson Tucker's the best mechanic in this area." He wraps his fireman's jacket around me, then he and the other fireman lift me onto a gurney. "Is there anybody else you want me to call?"

"No," I say.

Shouldn't women my age have at least ten

best friends on tap for situations like this? Both my parents are dead and nobody in Jackson was expecting me. The only person I can think of to call is my maid/personal assistant/jill-of-all-trades Roberta, and I sent her on vacation so I could make my getaway undetected. "There's no one."

"Don't you worry, Miss…"

"Gloria. Gloria Hart."

"Miss Hart, I'll be right there with you."

My lord, I'd forgotten how sweet Southern hospitality can be.

I wonder what else I've forgotten. I've been caught up for so long in the world of daytime television drama, I don't know the first thing about the real world.

He didn't have me at hello.

—Jenny

I'M UP TO my elbows in pie crust when the phone rings. Rick's cell phone number pops up and I refuse to answer it. There was a time when a phone call from Rick Miller would send me into a hormone-fueled tizzy, but now all I can think about is the passing of years that have left me with cellulite and crow's feet while my husband still looks like every woman's wet dream.

Considering our track record of the last few months, there's no way he's calling me in the middle of the day to propose something kinky or even mildly flirtatious. He's probably calling to see when I'll have the pies ready.

When he's not parading around in his volunteer fireman's uniform, Rick's running his little log-cabin restaurant under the hill and waiting for me to supply pies for the dessert menu.

I'm tired of pies.

"Up yours," I say, and my testy tone sends Rollo and Banjo scurrying under the table. Well, good. I'm also tired of keeping two dogs of dubious heritage happy—my other major daytime activity.

The phone keeps on ringing, so I finally give in and wipe the dough off my hands.

"Jenny, I've got a problem."

What happened to 'Hello, how are you?' I have problems, too, but I haven't lost my manners over it.

"Hello, Rick. How're you doing? Listen, I'm working on the pies, but they won't be ready for another hour."

"I'm not calling about pies. There was a wreck at the intersection."

"Who was hurt?"

I hope it's not a neighbor or one of my cousins. And though I've often said I wish she'd jump in a lake, I wouldn't even wish an accident on the mother-in-law from the Black Lagoon, Lulu Miller, who has hated me since Rick got serious. At every opportunity she opines I'm not good enough for her son, not smart enough and certainly not pretty enough.

Now Rick is telling me, "Some woman from California. Gloria Hart."

"Oh…my…*gosh*."

"Jenny? Are you all right?"

"Do you know who Gloria Hart is?"

"Yeah. I just told you. She wrecked her Italian sports car and banged up her leg."

"She's Jillian Rockwell from my favorite soap opera. Get her autograph."

There's a huge, deafening silence, and I wonder if Rick's cell phone has gone dead.

"Rick? Are you there?"

"This woman from California is in the emergency room without a single friend, and you want me to go up and ask for her autograph?"

"When you put it that way...look, I'm sorry, Rick. I wasn't thinking."

"Listen, her left ankle is bruised up and sprained and she'll be on a crutch a few days. There's no way she can manage alone in a motel. I was wondering if we could invite her to stay with us."

"Stay with us?"

The biggest soap-opera actress in Hollywood in my house, with a noisy, angst-ridden teenaged daughter, two spoiled hairy dogs and pie dough all over the kitchen counter?

"If you don't want to, maybe we can help her find a sitter."

"No. No, wait! Tell her she can stay with us. Oh...my...gosh!"

"Okay, then. We'll be home in time for supper."

I have to sit down. All of a sudden I've gone from an ordinary housewife covered in flour to an interesting woman with a Hollywood star sitting in my kitchen eating home-baked cherry pies.

Grabbing the dust mop and the Johnson's lemon wax, I go on a tornadic cleaning rampage that sends Rollo and Banjo into the master suite deep underneath the king-sized bed I can't remember using for anything but sleep in heaven knows when.

Oh, I know what all the slick women's magazines say about keeping romance alive, but I have enough to do keeping my seventeen-year-old daughter alive. Rick just got her a car and I just got my first gray hair.

Right now, though, I don't even have time to think about Angie. Important company's coming. A famous woman who has it all.

I stop my cleaning frenzy long enough to program the TV to tape *Love in the Fast Lane*, then I send a fervent prayer into the Universe.

"Help me remember Gloria Hart's a real person, just like me. Only eighty-five thousand times more glamorous."

Southern hospitality is not a myth.

—Gloria

LEANING HEAVILY on Rick and my new crutch in the middle of their charming country home, that's all I can say. If I say any more, I'll start bawling and won't be able to stop. Real tears. Not the fake kind.

I don't why, but unexpected kindness always undoes me. I can deal with a banged-up leg and having my car hauled off behind somebody who probably doesn't know beans about Italian sports cars. I can even deal with a younger woman stealing my TV spotlight. After all, I'm planning to steal it back.

But I don't know how I'm going to deal with ordinary life with Rick and Jenny Miller.

They have captured the American dream—marry, have a family, buy a house and two cars and live happily ever after. It's not my dream, but watching them, all smiles as they show me the spare bedroom where I'll be staying, I can't help but feel a bit cheated.

Back when I believed you could have it all, I tried twice to mix marriage with a career. Both times I failed miserably, which isn't all that uncommon when you consider the grim divorce statistics.

Of course, statistics are no consolation at all when you're dealing with a broken heart.

These two seem to have beaten the odds. It's going to be interesting to see how they do it.

CHAPTER 2

If I scream will I scare the cows?

—Gloria

When Rick and Jenny Miller told me to rest, that supper would be ready in a few hours, I was so keyed-up I didn't think I'd fall asleep.

Obviously, bruised bones are more painful and traumatic than I had imagined. Here I am, waking up in a four-poster bed underneath a pretty rose-sprigged canopy to the delicious aroma of Southern-fried chicken. The setting sun sends long slanting rays across the rocking chair in the corner, and children romping on a swing set across the street shout to one another as their mothers call them in to supper.

This reminds me of everything good about my childhood—the big kitchen where I could always find cookies in the jar, tall frosty glasses of lemonade, the rope swing on the big oak tree in the backyard where a homely little girl with buck teeth and thick glasses could dream of something more than the life of service the Catholic Sisters at Sacred Heart said was her destiny.

Somewhere in the Millers' house a raucous CD starts playing. I hear Jenny saying, "Angie, turn down the volume," and Angie's plaintive reply, "Aw, Mom."

There are footsteps, followed by a knock on my bedroom door.

"Come in."

Jenny cracks it open and peeps in. "How are you feeling?"

"Sore in places I didn't even know I had."

She slips inside holding a tray filled with every forbidden food on the planet—fried chicken, mashed potatoes, gravy, biscuits and peach cobbler with the crust floating in butter.

"I've made supper for you. I hope you're hungry."

"I think I've died and gone to heaven after all. I haven't had this many calories since I was sixteen."

"I can make you some soup. Or a light salad, or anything you want."

Oh, lord. She's going to treat me like a celebrity. I wish just once I could meet a woman who would get past what I do and consider me for who I am. Sometimes I think the only friend I have is Roberta, and that's only on her good days. She'll tell you in a New York minute—which is considerably shorter than a Mississippi minute—that most days she'd just as soon snatch me baldheaded as look at me.

"This looks great," I tell Jenny. "Southern comfort food, just like my mother used to make it."

"I forgot you were born in Jackson."

Jenny Miller stands there and spouts the Cinderella version of my history as reported in all the newspapers and slick magazines. Basically this is "homely country girl runs away from the Deep South and after the fairy godmothers of orthodontia and ophthalmology sprinkle her with fairy dust, she zooms to stardom."

The story is all glamour and hype. It leaves out my acting classes: the fast-food restaurant where I learned to act as if taking orders for hamburgers was preparation for running the country (and maybe it ought to be). Bay Street Boarding House where I feigned fifteen different illnesses to get my rent-due date extended. The department store where I sold more face cream than any other clerk by pretending to be twenty years older and sharing my beauty secret with women desperate to defy age and time.

I know, I know. I'm not a very admirable person. But listen, if you'd had a father waiting back home just itching to parcel out lectures on how to get your life on the right track and a mother who said I'd starve in Hollywood salivating for the opportunity to say, I told you so, wouldn't you resort to creativity?

A much nicer word than *lying*. And I do believe in the niceties.

I'm tempted to tell Jenny the real story, but most people prefer their fantasies to the truth. Besides, it's human nature to want heroes, especially if you've got one captured in your house. By remaining a mysterious star in Jenny's eyes, I give her bragging rights. It's the least I can do.

She sets the tray on my bed then adjusts the yellow rose in the small blue crystal vase on the edge of the tray. "Do you need anything else, Miss Hart?"

"Call me Gloria." I swallow my quip that Miss Hart makes me feel as old as my mother. She doesn't know about my warped sense of humor, and I don't want to hurt her feelings. "The rose is gorgeous. Did you grow it?"

"Yes. People say I have a green thumb."

"They're right."

"Miss…uh, Gloria, my daughter's back from swim practice and wants to meet you, but I told her she'd have to wait. I'm sure you don't feel like having company."

Polite people would show their gratitude by saying, let her come in, but my leg hurts like the devil and I'm not into martyrdom. Besides, I'm vain. After the drubbing I took in the rain in the ditch, I look like the wrong side of a baboon.

"Maybe tomorrow," I say.

"Can I get you anything else, or help you with anything?"

"If my crutch doesn't throw me, I'll be fine."

"Okay, then. I won't bother you again unless I hear a big thump on the floor."

I'm thankful that Jenny has a sense of humor. If I can figure out how to get her to loosen up, maybe I won't have to spend the next few days acting like fallen royalty being attended by loyal subjects.

She leaves and closes the door behind her. She's a pretty woman, not unlike the women I grew up with who devoted most of their time and effort to their families. Not enough makeup, a little too much fat around the middle, a touch of gray in her brown bob, oversized T-shirt over her jeans instead of a nice, crisp blue blouse that would bring out the color of her eyes.

She has a generous heart, too, something I've rarely seen in the last few years.

When Rick brought me here earlier in the afternoon, she said, "You can stay with us as long as you need to. Just make yourself at home. Our house is your house."

When I offered to pay for room and board, they turned me down flat. In fact, I think I insulted them. Unintentionally, of course. It's going to take me a while to remember all things Southern. Rule number one: when somebody does something nice for you, don't grab your pocketbook. Just say thank you.

I suppose I can regroup here as well as I could have in Jackson. The point never was to return to a place of bricks and mortar but to return to Mississippi. At least I'll be in a charming home filled with real people instead of a childhood home filled with ghosts.

After my parents drove their car into a train three years ago, I toyed with the idea of selling the house, but it's more than a house: it's my roots and my anchor. Although I rarely visit, I know the place is always there, my little piece of the Deep South, a reminder of where I started, how far I've come and who I am.

Thank the lord I don't have to worry about paying the bills till I can get my fighting boots back on, return to Hollywood and kick some serious butt.

As I grab a piece of chicken and crunch into the savory crust, I think how lucky I am. Really. I don't have what the Millers have—a loving partner to make the world feel safe and wonderful—but I do have the luxury of not having to worry about missing a few weeks work. Shoot, I could miss a few years and still be on solid financial ground. Of course, I have no intention of staying away from my work.

If Jenny keeps bringing me food like this I'll be up in no time and plotting a triumphant return to TV Land.

In the meantime I chow down on gravy and biscuits while real life unfolds outside my door.

I don't mean to eavesdrop. In spite of my character flaws, I haven't sunk that low. Still, when Rick and Jenny's voices float over the transom and through the walls, I can't help but hear.

"Don't wait up for me, Jen. I'll be working late at the restaurant tonight."

"Oh, Rick. Again?"

"You know how big the crowds are getting."

Jenny's husband kisses her. I can hear it plain as day, and all of a sudden I've lost interest in what they're saying.

I haven't had a kiss in five years that wasn't orchestrated by a TV director. And though I love acting, there are times when I long to be one of a pair, Mr. and Mrs. So-and-so with embroidered pillows on the bed, side by side. I don't know what it's like to have strong arms around me, and the sweet comfort of a man who understands that cuddling always makes things better.

I can't stand this. There's too much here to remind me of all the things I've lost. Or more precisely, never had.

Setting the tray on the bedside table, I ease out of bed and wobble toward the bathroom on my crutch. The nurses at the hospital sponged off the mud, but a good hot bath and a shampoo will make me feel better. Propping my crutch against the sink, I sit on the edge of the tub and unwrap the stretchy bandage from my ankle.

I'm glad it's time to take another pain pill. I hope it makes me sleep through all this marital bliss. If I have to hear the loving-couple sounds of Rick and Jenny Miller in the middle of the night, I won't be responsible for what I might do.

Screaming comes to mind.

Who stole my obedient daughter and turned her into a teenager?

—Jenny

WELL...there goes my drop-dead-gorgeous husband who could have women falling at his feet just by crooking his finger. And who knows? Maybe they do. Maybe that's why Rick has been working late every night for the last six months.

I can do two things: I can pitch a fit like my mother-in-law, Godzilla, which involves pouting and noisy tears followed by a few choice words that curl the ears of small dogs and innocent children. Or I can do what any normal under-appreciated, under-endowed housewife would do—

pick up the torch of civic duty and ramrod every women's club, charity benefit and cakewalk in Mooreville. Give me a telephone and a couple of days and I could get Banjo elected President. Of the United States, not the Mooreville Kennel Club.

As I march toward the telephone, I detour to Angie's room. Sprawled on the bed with the telephone growing from her ear, she's dark, long-limbed and gorgeous. Just like her daddy.

"Angie." I can recognize a guilty jump a mile away. "You're not talking to Jackson Tucker, are you?"

"No." A bald-faced lie. I can tell by the way she widens her big brown eyes. "I was talking to Sally. About going to the library tomorrow morning."

Angie reading? In the summer? No way.

"Great. Maybe you can get a headstart on some of your senior English reading."

"Sure thing, Mom." She twists her long black ponytail around her finger and gives me a radiant smile. Another gift from her father. I swear, let these two smile at you and you're putty in their hands.

Any other time and I'd call her bluff. No seventeen-year-old should be fooling around with a twenty-five-year-old, I don't care how good he is at fixing cars. Especially a wild buck like Jackson Tucker. But I'm not going to start a family ruckus in front of Gloria Hart, of all people.

"Hurry up and finish the call, Angie. I need to make a few calls about the barbecue at Tuck's."

Yet another charity benefit after I swore to Rick I'd cut back. But this is for a good cause, one he should appreciate—the volunteer fire department.

Life would be simpler if we had two phone lines. Angie's been lobbying for her own for two years, and Rick wants to get it for her. I lost the argument about getting her a car, but I'm holding firm about the phone. I was brought up to believe you ought to earn your way, that life doesn't get handed to you on a silver platter. If I left the child-raising decisions to Rick, he'd already have given Angie Mexico City wrapped in a gold ribbon with Tijuana thrown in for good measure.

The minute I turn my back, Angie says into the phone, "Bye. Gotta go."

Another clear sign she's defying me by carrying on her dangerous flirtation with a young man who's far too old and worldly wise for her. I swear, he is so busy racing around on his motorcycle I don't know how he runs a garage and repair shop.

Well, actually I do. With help from his daddy. Matt Tucker (Tuck, we call him) can fix anything except his own lonely life.

Who am I to talk? I can't fix my boxed-in, disappointing life, either.

When our marriage started out, I was Rick's right-hand woman, not only his loving wife but his helpmate in his fledgling restaurant. I was acting as hostess, booking little private parties for the banquet room and helping in the office. Then one day, the cook got sick and I pitched in. One taste of my pies, and the customers were hooked.

After Angie was born, I moved pie-making operations to the house, and the rest is history. I'm here, Rick's there, and nothing's in between. We hardly ever see each other except to say, "Pass the biscuits."

Now I take the portable kitchen phone off its base then fix a big bowl of peach cobbler with ice cream to nibble while I call my best friend Laurel. I might as well. What's another pound or two? And who notices, anyhow? Certainly not my husband.

"You'll never guess who's staying at my house." When I tell her about Gloria, she squeals like a teenager. This is one of the things I love most about her: in spite of holding the staid position as director of the Lee County Library, in spite of being an icon to the community, she's still a little girl at heart.

Laurel demands full details, and after I promise to make sure she gets to meet Gloria, I take a big bite of cobbler, let the comfort of peaches and cream settle on my tongue and my thighs, then dial the first of fifty people on my list. Thank goodness, this will take a while. Long enough for me to have another helping of peach cobbler with maybe some toasted English walnuts on the side and forget that the black silk nightgown I bought on my fortieth birthday last September is going to waste in my bedroom closet.

I had such hopes for that gown. Visions of me wrapped in my husband's arms in a state of connubial bliss.

What has happened to us? All I've ever wanted was to be loved by Rick Miller.

Banjo slides under the table and licks my ankle

while Rollo sits at the base of my chair and puts his head on my knee.

At least the dogs love me.

Maybe I'm wrong. Maybe Rick does still love me. Maybe he'll surprise me and come home early tonight.

I turn my full attention to the telephone and the peach cobbler.

At nine-thirty I fold my list, put the phone in its cradle and join Angie in the den where she's watching *Tristan and Isolde* on HBO.

The clock inches toward eleven while hope fades. I take a tissue from the box and cry over the fate of star-crossed lovers everywhere.

When did Mom start riding a broomstick?

—Angie

I CAN IDENTIFY with this movie. As far as I'm concerned, Tristan and Isolde could be Jackson and me with warring separate nations trying to keep us apart. Not that Mom's a warring nation, but when she gets on her high horse—which happens all the time lately—you feel like she's sicced an army on you, got you bound and gagged and thrown in the dungeon waiting to get your head chopped off.

She's says I'm overly dramatic, but she's the one who wanted me to be the star of all the school plays. What did she expect?

Now here she is hogging all the popcorn and acting like my best buddy when I know good and well she's plotting to keep Daddy from getting me a cell phone. Or anything else I want that shows I'm growing up.

Why can't she see I'm not a little girl anymore? She was practically married at my age, and if there's a more wonderful man than my daddy, I don't know who. If Mom was old enough when she was in high school to pick him out, why can't I?

We've come to the good part of the movie now—I've seen it a dozen times—where Tristan and Isolde get back together. Secretly, of course. This part always makes me cry. And want butter.

Naturally when I reach for the popcorn all I get is a few hard kernels. Mom's hogged it all and is sitting over there on her side of the couch sniffing into a tissue, acting like she sympathizes with their plight.

She wouldn't understand star-crossed lovers if you tattooed it on her forehead. She's too busy trying to keep me from growing up.

I wish she could be more like Sally's mom. Mrs. Talant lifts Sally's curfew on weekends. She's not on her case about everything, either. Last week when Sally and I smoked in her bedroom, I know good and well her mom smelled the smoke, even though we took turns standing at the open window and fanning. But she didn't say a word.

Mom would have stormed in there acting like we'd committed a cardinal sin. She'd have spent ten minutes lecturing us about lung cancer and premature babies. I know her like a book.

The only thing she's done to surprise me lately is let a real Hollywood actress stay with us. I haven't met her yet, but Dad said she was driving a Ferrari and that she took her wreck like a champ.

See, that's what I'm talking about. Why can't Mom take a few things in stride?

I'm hoping Miss Hart stays long enough so some of her joie de vivre will rub off on Mom.

I feel so cool knowing that expression. Maybe Mom ought to take French.

Is Squirt still a term of endearment, or is it merely the sound mustard makes when it spews out of the bottle and all over your blouse?

—Jenny

NOISES IN MY HOUSE wake me at 4:00 a.m.

I turn to wake Rick, but his side of the bed is empty. Either he didn't come home last night or he's gone to the kitchen to get a snack or even put on the coffee. An insomniac, he has a tendency to prowl the house at all hours.

Putting on my faded summer seersucker robe and terry-cloth slippers, I tiptoe through the semi-darkness toward the light burning in the kitchen.

And that's when I hear my husband's voice and the unmistakable sultry drawl of daytime TV's most beautiful femme fatale.

Rick is leaning against the stove by the coffeepot, smiling, while Gloria sits at the kitchen table, her crutch propped against her chair and her long blond hair flowing down the back of an elaborately bejeweled and embroidered red silk dressing gown. It probably cost more than my Chevrolet pickup.

A woman has no right to look that incredible at four in the morning without a stitch of makeup, especially in front of my husband, who is clearly appreciating every minute of this kitchen rendezvous.

The green-eyed monster waylays me with such force I feel like bopping Rick on the head with the coffeepot. Instead I stand in the doorway—unnoticed, might I add—until I can get my unexpected jealousy under control.

After all, I'm being ridiculous. Why in the world would Hollywood's glamour queen have the slightest interest in a small-town man of modest means who has never done anything more exciting than score the winning goal to cinch the state championship for his high school's basketball team?

That doesn't take into account our honeymoon in Las Vegas where he lit every one of my lights.

And they haven't gone out since.

On the other hand, Gloria has stolen three husbands and brought two kings to their knees. Of course, that's her TV persona, Jillian Rockwell, but still, there was that real-life scandal with the famous movie director.

You never know how closely art imitates life.

"Oh, I'm so sorry," she says. "I seem to have awakened the entire house."

Standing there feeling like a toad I note that everything about her is gorgeous, from the top of her lustrous blond hair to the tips of her perfectly manicured nails. Not to mention she's wearing an emerald ring as big as my head.

The pocket of my robe is ripped and the seat is worn almost threadbare. I feel like a bag of rumpled laundry. A *jealous* bag.

"She came in to get some ice just as I was coming home," Rick says.

He was just coming home? *This* is supposed to make me feel better?

"After I closed the restaurant I was doing accounts and fell asleep over the books."

First Angie lies about Jackson and now Rick makes up this flimsy story. Is everybody in my family conspiring to make me look foolish in front of a woman I've cheered for, wept with, idolized and secretly envied every day at noon for the last twenty years?

"Oh," is all I can say.

I feel naked standing in the door with my feelings showing all over my face. After all, I'm no Emmy-award-winning actress.

Gloria grabs her crutch and stands. Towers is

more like it. Even in bare feet she's at least four inches taller than my five feet five inches. And about a million times sexier.

"I'd better get back to my bedroom so everybody can sleep."

Rick watches her hobble out, then turns off the coffeepot. I guess it would have been fun to drink coffee with Gloria. I guess I'm just chopped liver.

He drapes his arm around my shoulder and squeezes.

"Let's go to bed, Squirt."

That's been his nickname for me since he first saw me in the sandbox at Ballard Park. I was two and he was four. The name became public knowledge when I stood on the sidelines in my pleated cheerleader's skirt and pom-poms shouting into a megaphone so everybody in the Mooreville High School gymnasium would cheer for the basketball star. As he dribbled the ball past me, he shouted, "You tell 'em, Squirt."

I used to love that name. Now I'm hoping Gloria didn't hear it. I'm wishing he'd call me something else. Darling. Sweetheart. Precious.

If I thought I was precious to Rick Miller, I'd die a happy woman.

In the bedroom we lie side by side not touching, not even our hips.

"Are you okay, Squirt?"

"Sure."

I know I ought to shut up and go to sleep. I know heated words spoken at 4:00 a.m. can lead to regret in the bright light of day. But it's like picking a sore you know is going to bleed. You just can't let it alone.

"So, you slept slumped over a desk all night?"

"Yes."

"You didn't get a crick in your neck? Your legs didn't go to sleep all scrunched up under the desk? You didn't even have to get up to pee?"

"Jen, do you know how that sounds? Just let it alone. You're imagining things."

"Maybe I need a brain transplant."

I'm on a roll here. There are all kinds of cutting things I can say about him making coffee before daylight for a woman who can mesmerize a nation with one look from her incredible violet eyes.

But Rick puts his hand on my thigh, and I hold my breath, waiting, hoping. Finally I can no longer stand the suspense.

"Does this mean the dry spell is over?"

"'Night, Jen."

Rick rolls over and turns his back to me.

Great. I can't let well enough alone. I can't swallow my pride long enough to accept a little peace offering. I have to be a snippy hog, mad because six months of strangers-in-the-same-bed didn't get wiped out in one big passionate hurrah.

We were going to be the kind of couple who always had something to say to each other across the breakfast table, the kind who greeted each other at the end of a day's work as if we'd been separated by war, the kind who fed each other popcorn at the movies even after we had to get bifocals to see the box.

Lying there with my hopes dashed and my dreams shattered, I watch the clock inch toward morning.

I wish I could trade lives with Gloria.

CHAPTER 3

Can a good coat of gloss fix this mess? And I'm not talking lip gloss.

—Gloria

Clearly Jenny Miller thinks I'm after her husband.

As Roberta would say if she were here, I should have kept my skinny butt in bed and not acted like my every whim was an edict from God. Who needs ice at four o'clock in the morning?

In my own defense, twenty years of being in the studio at the crack of dawn to get my hair and makeup done for the show have left me with an internal clock that jars me awake when no self-respecting rooster would be up.

Pulling the covers under my chin, I try to sleep, but that's impossible. Sure, Rick Miller's good-looking, but nothing would tempt me to play fast and loose with the husband of a woman who is sharing her house and upending her entire routine for me.

The only way I can fix this mess is to convince her I'm a woman to trust. Spread a little charm around. Shoot, I'm good at this. After all, I'm one of a dying breed, a true Southern belle. Beauty—thanks to good orthodontia and Max Factor—and a backbone of steel.

Nothing gets the best of me. Certainly not a little setback with my hostess.

When I hear Rick leave the house at eight, I drag myself out of bed, grab my ridiculously expensive designer robe, then ditch it in favor of a multi-colored peasant skirt and pink off-the-shoulder blouse. My favorite gold dangly earrings and bangle bracelets. Minimum makeup, just a touch of mascara and lip gloss.

Shoot. I feel as stiff as a ninety-five-year-old. Plus, the bruise on my left hip has grown to the size of Mount Everest. As Roberta would say, I ought to count my blessings. Except the only blessing I can think of is that nobody is going to ask me to pose for a magazine layout in a bikini.

I hobble my way to the kitchen where Jenny

is up to her elbows in dough while two dogs sit at her feet with their tongues lolled out and their tails thumping.

"Hi," she says. "How are you feeling this morning?"

She's a terrible actress, all fake smiles and false cheer. I could sit down and match her, lie for lie. We could dance around each other all morning, and never say anything of real substance.

That's the easy way. Just pretend everything's okay and go on about our business.

But I didn't get to be the goddess of daytime TV by doing things the easy way. I plop into the chair, my sprained ankle making me as graceful as a mule, then haul off and aim for the heart of the matter.

"Look, Jenny, I know you probably see me as some big-shot celebrity trying to add another notch to my belt with your very handsome husband, but believe me, that's as far from the truth as it gets."

Jenny pounds the dough harder. "Oh, I didn't think for a minute you had ulterior motives."

Even the dogs don't believe her. Their tails stop wagging, and they cock their heads as if to say, "That's a bunch of bull."

"No, but I'll bet you thought Rick did."

"Well, of course I..." Jenny pulls her hands out of the dough, wipes them on her apron and pours two cups of coffee. "You know what? That's exactly what I thought. You're famous and glamorous while I'm plain and dull. How could he not be tempted?"

She sets the coffee between us, and we both assess each other as we sip. What I'm seeing is a woman not too sure of herself who is trying to figure out if I'm just playing another role or if I'm sincere.

"Jenny, if you believe half the things that have been written about me, then you must think I'm a spoiled, rich woman with a staff catering to my every whim and men groveling for the privilege of touching the hem of my skirt."

"Leave out the spoiled part, and that's about right."

"Wrong. Contrary to the reports that I kicked both my husbands out, my first husband moved in with an older actress who had more clout and could do more to advance his career, and the second one developed a fondness for bars featuring men in silk stockings and beaded bustiers."

"*They* left *you?*"

"*Dumped* is a better word. And that story about the married studio head was nothing but the pipe dream of an over-eager reporter who saw us drinking champagne together at a crowded New Year's Eve party and turned the incident into a sex scandal."

"I remember the headlines. The Goddess and the Movie Lion."

Spontaneous laughter with another woman feels so good. I'm glad I crashed my car in a place that's little more than a cow pasture. Real people live here. Not Tinsel Town mannequins whose every move is scripted to gain the attention of the press and capture an audience with the movie producer who has the backing of the richest studio.

"I hate that term. *Goddess*. Roberta says it makes me sound like a salad dressing."

"Green goddess?"

"Something like that."

While Jenny refills our coffee cups and gets two fat muffins off a platter, I tell her about Roberta, who was slaving away unnoticed and unappreciated in the studio's secretarial pool before I snatched her up and put her to work as my personal assistant, lonely hearts advisor, bodyguard and friend.

"You name it, and Roberta fills the bill. Of course, I pay her handsomely. She probably wouldn't give me the time of day if I didn't." I take a bite of my muffin before I start sounding like one of those women who love to wallow in angst and self-pity. "Actually the fact that I pay her to do something she loves is a running joke between us. These muffins are delicious. Homemade?"

"They are. People say I'm the best baker in Mooreville. Maybe even the whole state."

"I wish I could cook."

"You want to learn to cook?"

"Yes. Apparently, it really is the way to a man's heart. Just look at you and Rick."

"Looks can be deceiving." Jenny gets up. Fast. A signal that I've moved into territory where she's posted a keep-out sign. "Listen, I'm available for whatever you want to do today. Whatever you feel like doing."

"I don't want to disrupt your life. Just go about your business and I'll try not to get in the way."

"Well, let me see. I doubt that I can make pies with an audience, and I certainly don't think I can keep two mutts entertained while you're around."

Jenny's smiling, but I can hear the sting of truth behind her quips. She feels trapped in a life

I perceive as the American dream, while I'm leading a high-stress, competitive, brutally lonely life she sees as glamorous and desirable.

"By the way, this is Rollo." Jenny leans down to pet the big shaggy brown dog on the head. "And this little runt is Banjo."

He's no bigger than a squirrel, and twice as fast. Before I know what's happening Banjo has jumped into my lap and is licking my emerald as if it's a mint drop.

Or maybe he knows it's my good-luck charm. I bought it after I landed my role as Jillian. Shamrock green for luck. Green light for go. A reminder to myself to keep charging forward.

"Banjo! Down!" Jenny scoops him off my lap, but I'm laughing so hard I can barely catch my breath.

"I haven't had that much attention from a male in five years."

"You've got to be kidding."

"Oh, no. Those passionate kisses you see in *Love in the Fast Lane* are nothing more than good camera angles and lots of breath mints."

A teenaged girl appears in the doorway sporting black lipstick and a big attitude. Jenny introduces me to her daughter, and Angie, who apparently suffers none of her mother's shaky self-esteem, pours herself a bowl of cereal, then plops into the chair next to mine.

"Cool. Can I see that Italian sports car Daddy said you were driving?"

"Angie!" Jenny says, but I'm relieved that at least one member of this household is not in awe of anything except my car.

"As a matter of fact, I was hoping I could visit the mechanic today and ask about my car."

Angie perks up. "Jackson?"

"I don't even know. I guess I was in shock when your daddy called the garage."

Angie jumps up, her cereal forgotten. "I'll drive you over."

"I thought you and Sally were going to the library this morning," Jenny says.

An unspoken challenge passes between mother and daughter. I don't know what this is all about, but I'm right in the middle of it. A pawn in this game of control they're playing.

"Sally will understand. Besides, you're *cooking*."

"In this house, we honor our commitments."

Stiff with self-righteous indignation, Angie

empties her bowl into the sink. And when she turns on the garbage disposal, she lets the loud grinding go on way past the time it would take to pulverize soggy cereal.

"It was nice to meet you, Miss Hart." She turns a radiant smile in my direction, then glares at her mother and makes a stormy exit that would rival some of my best on *Love in the Fast Lane*.

"Well..." Jenny lifts her shoulders and speaks with faux cheer. "If you feel like riding over, I'll drive you to see about your car. As soon as I finish getting these pies assembled."

"Thanks, I'd like that. I'm a bit stiff, but other than that, I feel fine. I guess all those yoga classes have finally paid off."

"Okay, then." Distracted, Jenny glances at the doorway where Angie has now vanished.

It's time for me to get out of the way and let her handle her daughter. Angie reminds me of myself as a teenager. Headstrong and defiant, always testing authority and skirting danger.

Maybe the gods of love everlasting knew what they were doing when they broke up my two marriages. I don't know how I would have handled a demanding career and a problem child.

"I think I'll lie down and prop my leg up until you're ready to go."

As I clump off on my crutch, I'm thinking the American dream looks more flawed by the minute. Still, couldn't I have at least been sprinkled with stardust from the gods of mind-boggling sex?

Where was the sign that said Sharp Curves Ahead, Dangerous to All Relationships, and how did I miss it?

—Jenny

WHILE Gloria and Angie leave, I'm standing here with murder on my mind. I don't know who will be first—my husband or my daughter. Lately, they're both intent on driving me insane. I wish I could just climb into my truck and drive off. I don't care where. Anywhere but here.

Instead, I finish assembling the pies, watch out the window while Angie peels off toward Sally's on two wheels, make a mental note to tattle to Rick, which is about all it will amount to. There's no discussing Angie with him. In his eyes she's perfect, even in the case of Jackson Tucker. Rick says we ought to trust her enough to let her find out for herself if Jackson's right for her. He says the more I forbid her to see him, the more determined Angie will be.

I say we're the parents, we should make the rules. I might as well be whistling into a hurricane.

What do I know? A woman who was raised by parents who guided me with tough love, God rest their souls. While Rick, of course, ran loose under the evil eye of the Mother from the Black Lagoon.

I shove the pies into the refrigerator so I can bake them when we get back from the garage. Then I wash the dough off my hands, brush my hair, toy with the idea of lipstick but decide my face is hopeless, and knock on Gloria's door.

"I'm ready," she says.

When she comes out, I guess I stand there tongue-tied because she starts laughing.

"Jenny, I won't bite and I bleed like real people. Honestly."

"I just can't get over seeing you in the flesh, that's all. I've worshipped you from afar for twenty years. Having you here is like a dream."

As incredible as it sounds, she seems to be

trying really hard to be my friend. I wonder if that's possible. Plain, ordinary, unexciting, small-town Jenny Miller, friends with the biggest soap star in the nation?

"I'm sorry about Angie's behavior this morning."

"Don't apologize. I was young once."

"You look about thirty."

"Can I take you back to Hollywood and let you tell that to the director who canned me?"

"You're off the show? That's unbelievable."

"Yes. But not for long. I don't take defeat lying down."

I wish I didn't. I almost say this aloud to Gloria, but my life pales beside hers. What's a teenager—and maybe even a husband—running wild compared to a successful acting career?

"I'm driving a truck. Do you think you can climb in?"

"One advantage of long legs is being able to get into pickup trucks."

I hold her crutch while she catches the strap and swings up.

"I figured you rode around in limousines all the time."

"Jenny, my life is not as glamorous as you'd think. And sometimes I'd chuck every bit of it for even a small part of what you have."

After Angie's display in the kitchen, she's clearly not talking about having a teenaged daughter. That leaves Rick. Obviously she has us confused with one of Hollywood's classic love matches. Gable and Lombard. And who knows if that would have lasted if Lombard hadn't died young in a plane crash.

I have no intention of dying young. What I've got to do is figure out how to make my husband notice me again without becoming the idolized dead.

Pulling out of the driveway I head south on Highway 371.

"The garage is only five miles down the road," I tell Gloria. "Jackson Tucker's daddy gave him the land, which was once part of Tuck's Farms."

"My lord. Matt Tucker, the thoroughbred trainer?"

It doesn't surprise me that she knows of him. Matt's the best breeder and trainer in the country and at one time or another has been written up in *Racing World* and all the big magazines. And according to Laurel, who knows about such things thanks to her two divorces, he's also the most eligible bachelor in the Deep South.

"He's the one. Jackson is a genius with his hands. I don't know whether his daddy is keeping him nearby so he can fix the Tuck's Farms equipment or so he can keep an eye on him. Jackson's wilder than a March hare. Angie thinks she's in love with him."

"I see."

Thank goodness she's not the kind to pry. I'm so glad to be out of the kitchen, I don't want to talk about my petty problems. I want to escape them, to kick up my heels and pretend we're good friends on a morning outing that might end with the two of us trying on dresses at Reed's or selecting new linens at T.J. Maxx.

When I pull up at the garage, Jackson emerges from under the hood of a blue Ferrari and runs around to open Gloria's door.

As far as I know, he's never opened a door for anybody in his life.

"You must be Gloria Hart. T.V. doesn't do you justice."

He's flirting with her. The little twerp. Of

course, what red-blooded man wouldn't? Still, when he bends over and kisses her hand, I want to boot him in the seat of the pants. I've told Rick and Angie he chases everything in skirts. She says I'm being picky, that nobody she dates would be good enough to suit me, and Rick says Jackson's just being charming. Like his mother.

Well, we all know how that turned out. Jolene Beaumont-Tucker was a famous opera singer and charming to everybody—the press who loved to ride out to Tuck's Farms and take pictures of her in that getup she wore in *Madame Butterfly*, the cadre of maids she required to wait on her hand and foot, the stable boys, her personal trainer. Some say she was especially charming to her personal trainer, though as far as I'm concerned, that's just a vicious rumor.

All I *do* know is that she was charming to everybody but her husband. I've heard her shoot verbal barbs at Matt in front of two hundred people milling around their backyard eating Fourth of July barbecue.

Rick thinks Jackson's bound to have his daddy's finer qualities, but I'm here to tell you, that boy's apple fell straight from his mother's warped tree.

Gloria deftly pulls her hand away from Jackson, which shoots her up another notch on my decency scale. She already went up there around sainthood when she assured me she's not interested in stealing my husband.

"Jenny brought me to get a first-hand report of the damage," she tells Jackson.

"I had to order parts, but I've already started the body work. I'll show you."

She matches him stride for stride, no mean feat on her crutch, while I hang back and watch him show off in his muscle shirt. He knows about body work, all right. Tucker got every bit of his daddy's good looks.

But he doesn't fool Gloria for a minute. She controls the conversation as if she'd written the script. And she's keeping it strictly business.

Speaking of good looks, Matt Tucker himself gallops this way.

Matt and Gloria spot each other at the same time. When he reins his stallion to a halt in front of her it's like watching that exquisite moment in the movies when the hero and heroine first meet. They melt into each other's gazes and you just know they're going to end up riding off into the sunset and living happily ever after.

Wouldn't it be wonderful if life could turn out that way? If husbands and wives could keep their love new and exciting till their dying day, and even after death find their way back to each other through time and space?

It's not happening for me, of course, but that doesn't stop me from believing other people can have that kind of magic. Especially people as talented and gorgeous as Tuck and Gloria.

And might I add, deserving. Tuck's been alone for twenty years, ever since that high-falutin' Jolene stormed back to her career in New York and left him with a five-year-old son. He devoted himself to raising Jackson and the best thoroughbred horses in the country. As far as anybody knows, he never even came close to finding another woman to love.

Thinking that I could be the catalyst for what might turn out to be another Gable/Lombard romance of the century gives me goose bumps.

"Gloria, I'd like you to meet my neighbor, Matt Tucker. Tuck, this is Gloria Hart. She's a television star and my friend."

Oh my gosh, how presumptuous of me. And yet, the warm smile Gloria turns in my direction tells me it might be so. We might sit on the bed with a big bowl of popcorn between us while I bare my soul. Will my handsome husband leave me for a more exciting woman? Will my daughter keep her head on her shoulders, or will she throw away her virginity without thought to the future?

Husbands and teenagers should come with instructions.

CHAPTER 4

When life imitates art, should you run away or stay and celebrate?

—Gloria

My lord, has Mooreville cornered the market on sexy men?

Dark-eyed and dangerous-looking in an honest-to-goodness cowboy hat, Matt Tucker makes my former leading man on *Love in the Fast Lane* look like milquetoast.

I focus on his hands. They are beautiful, with long, tapered fingers. The sight affects me in some deep-seated, visceral way. I can imagine them making erotic circles on my flesh.

"Miss Hart." Tuck acknowledges me with nothing more than a quick nod of his head, and all of sudden, I don't care what he thinks and what his hands look like. His greeting is dismissive. As if I'm not even worth a smile.

Nothing gets my dander up more than being summarily dismissed. If I weren't on this crutch I'd show him dismissive. I'd be so imperious he'd thank his lucky stars he escaped with his head.

"Mr. Tucker." I give him an equally curt nod. Let that arrogant Mississippi cowboy think I'm not impressed. Let him think any darned thing he wants.

"I think we're finished here, Jenny. And my leg's beginning to hurt a little."

"Oh, then we'll head home." Jenny turns back to Tuck. "Good to see you."

"You, too, Jenny. I'll call later about the benefit."

Finally he smiles, and I see why he's so grudging with them. Good lord, if he smiled at me the way he's smiling at Jenny I'd probably grovel and beg him to handle me the way he's handling that thoroughbred.

I sweep toward Jenny's pickup with a modicum of grace and style. In spite of my crutch. In spite of the sting of another rejection. Though why I'm comparing Matt Tucker to my ex-husbands is beyond my comprehension.

As I slump into the seat, I realize the sting is

not to my pride but to my spirit. No matter how much I enjoy my career, I still yearn for the lovely soul connection that sprinkles stardust on everything else. To glimpse that possibility and have those hopes dashed tears a little hole in the spirit.

"The very idea," Jenny says.

"Indeed."

"I should have thought about your leg."

"I'm not talking about my leg. I'm talking about that hunk of arrogant male attitude masquerading as a real person. Blue jeans and T-shirts that tight ought to be declared against the law."

"I know. Jackson's a pissant."

"Wrong Tucker."

"Matt?"

"Yeah, Matt. Who does he think he is? King of the Universe?"

"Why, he's just as humble as apple pie."

"Not from where I was standing."

"Oh…my…gosh."

"What?"

"You fell for him."

"You've got to be kidding. A man without enough manners to get off his horse?" This is pride talking.

"Those thoroughbreds are high-strung. Matt never turns over the reins to anybody except one of the stable boys."

"He probably never turns over the reins of anything. His wife must be a doormat."

I'm fishing here. I can't remember what I read about his marital status. And after all, a married man could leave his wedding ring at home, especially a man like Matt Tucker dealing with high-strung thoroughbreds all day.

"His wife left him."

"I can see why." Jenny twists around and gives me this *look*, and my face flushes. "Okay, you caught me red-handed."

The choice is mine. Protect myself with flippancy or open myself to pain with the truth. I opt for the truth, to solidify a blossoming friendship.

"So, what did you really think?"

"I can't believe any woman would leave him. I've never met a man that sexy outside a studio. Or that appealing. My lord, in Hollywood he'd be box-office gold."

"When you first saw each other, the temperature went so high I thought my hair was going to catch on fire."

Jenny drives along in silence, probably trying to figure out if I'm acting. I never knew my profession could be such a handicap. Of course, I should have. It probably contributed heavily to the breakup of my marriages, and it has certainly kept me from forming close ties with other women.

Other actresses view me as competition, and women leading less hectic, less glamorous lives can't imagine they'd ever have anything in common with me.

What they don't see is an ordinary woman longing for the kind of wonderful friendship where either party could pick up the phone in the middle of the night to say, "I'm hurting," and the other would rush over with hugs and Hershey bars.

When we arrive at Jenny's house, she says, "Would you mind if I invited Tuck to dinner?"

"Tonight?"

"Not tonight. But sometime soon. When you're feeling better."

"Are you matchmaking?"

She laughs. "I guess you could call it that. But I just think there's something between you and Tuck so powerful it would be a sin to ignore it."

I believe in fate. When you consider the thousand-plus miles I traveled before I wrecked my car, shouldn't there be a reason other than a large black-and-white cow—or dog—in the road? Isn't it possible I was supposed to land in this exact spot in Mississippi to find the two people who could rescue me? A good friend to lift me up when my wings are too bedraggled to fly and a good man to be my haven at the end of a hard day in the Hollywood trenches?

Jenny parks the truck in the shade of a magnolia tree and we sit there a minute, letting the morning's events sink in.

Finally she says, "I have to bake pies."

"I'm going to rest a while. My ankle really is throbbing."

"I'll make some sweet tea for you to take to your room."

Sweet tea. I haven't heard that expression since my childhood. I'm flooded with memories of golden days filled with dreams of fame, fortune and love.

Two out of three's not bad.

We go into the house and Jenny pours the tea into a tall glass of ice. Heading into the bedroom to stretch out on the rose-sprigged comforter while the ceiling fan stirs the air, I wonder what sort of dreams I can conjure now.

Laundry ought to come with warning signs: beware of chapped hands and broken hearts.

—Jenny

WHILE Gloria rests I stick the pies in the oven and get Rick's jeans out of the dirty clothes hamper to do laundry. The house is quiet with Rick at the restaurant and Angie at the library with Sally—I hope. If she's not there, I don't even want to think about where she might be or what she might be doing.

When I was her age I had only one thing on my mind—how to get Rick Miller to notice me.

Funny, but after twenty-something years, that's still the main thing on my mind.

With the rich smells of pecan and lemon meringue pies wafting from the kitchen, I dig through Rick's pockets. He's notorious for leaving behind little things: loose change, lug nuts, small screws, wadded-up tissue.

Now I pull out two nails, a penny and some scraps of paper. I toss the nails into the garbage and put the penny in the loose-change jar I keep by the washing machine, then unfold the notes to see if they're anything important. The first one says milk, sugar, coffee—the list I gave him last Tuesday when he was going into town.

The second one is on pink paper. Sylvia, 310-788-0009.

I catch a whiff of something and lift the note to my nose. Chanel No. 5. I used to wear that fragrance eighteen years ago BC—before children, before cellulite, before crazy-making days like this one.

What kind of woman gives a man her phone number on pink scented paper? The kind who is up to no good with my husband. That's what.

Moving on automatic, I dump Rick's pants into the machine and reach for the detergent while an old song plays in my head. "I'm Gonna Wash that Man Right Outta my Hair."

Of course, it's not my hair that's dirty. It's my husband. And here I stand washing his two-timing pants.

Jerking the cheating britches out of the machine, I throw them on the floor and stomp on them.

Rollo and Banjo come running, hackles up, ready to attack the dangerous intruder. The only problem is, Sylvia's not here. She's probably in my husband's office capturing him with her scented talons.

When the dogs see me stomping Rick's pants, they come to a screeching halt and tilt their heads sideways as if to say, "We knew she was headed around the bend. We just didn't know it would happen this fast."

All I want is out of this house.

Grabbing my gardening gloves, hat and a pair of sharp clippers, I head to the rose garden with the dogs at my heels and start lopping off dead heads. Spent blooms that must be removed in order to make way for the new ones.

I'm a superb gardener, a Master Gardener, in fact. I took the course and became active in their organization. It's another one of the many ways I fill my spare time.

Thanks to the restaurant, the volunteer fire department and love-starved women penning passionate notes on love-colored paper, I have more spare time than a wife with a good-looking husband ought to have.

What I ought to have is lots of stolen moments with Rick behind the closed doors of his office in broad daylight, passionate kisses in the gazebo under a full moon, and some old-fashioned making-out underneath the rose arbor in the secluded corner of the yard.

Apparently *I'm* a spent bloom, as shriveled-up and colorless as the dried-out roses hitting the ground.

When I finish dead-heading I start snipping fresh blooms. Nothing lifts the spirit like roses all over the house. I'll put the creamy Peace roses in the dining room, the yellow Sun Sprite in the living room and the rose-colored Gertrude Jekyll in the bedroom. The Gertrude Jekyll smells like French perfume. Maybe the fragrance will be enough to take Rick's mind off Sylvia.

This very minute she's probably tripping around in her four-inch sling-backs picking out a cute little cottage they'll turn into a love nest after the divorce is final.

Well, I have news for that vixen. I'm not fixing to lie down and play dead. I'm going to use every weapon in my arsenal to hold onto my man.

Gathering my roses I head back to the house.

The minute I open the back door, I'm hit by the sound of the fire alarm and a face full of smoke.

Dropping the roses on the utility-room floor, I barrel into the kitchen with the dogs barking at my heels.

"Jenny. Thank goodness." Gloria's standing in the smoke waving a dish towel.

It's not enough that I've nearly burned the house down; I've nearly asphyxiated the goddess of daytime TV.

"I've turned the oven off," she says, "but the pies are still in there. This darned crutch!"

I jerk the charred remains out of the oven then fling open windows while Gloria swats at the smoke.

"Jenny!"

Just what I need. Rick. Home to get the pies.

Suddenly he's standing in the kitchen door and I don't know whether to hug him or kill him.

"Good God."

He picks Gloria up and carries her off, leaving me in the kitchen to die of smoke inhalation. Of course, I'm glad he got Gloria out of harm's way, but wouldn't you think he'd want to save his wife from death by charred pie?

Here I stand. Second choice. Actually third when you consider that husband-snatcher, Sylvia.

Even the dogs have deserted me. They're trailing along behind Rick, barking.

"Don't just stand there, Jenny," he yells over his shoulder. "Get out. I'll take care of the smoke."

I throw the dish towel on the floor and trail along behind them to the front porch. He sets Gloria on the chaise so she can prop up her leg, then passes me on his way back to the kitchen.

"What happened?" he says.

"Don't ask."

I pull up a rocking chair and sit down beside Gloria.

"Are you okay?" I ask.

"I'm fine. Don't worry about me."

"I don't do this every day. Flambé the pies, behead all my roses. Stomp Rick's pants."

"You stomped his pants?"

I might as well quit pretending. I need help. Of course I can call Laurel, but she's at work and I need a confidante *now*.

"Actually, Gloria, the thing I'd like to send up in flames is Rick."

Forget that my husband's in the kitchen. Let him deal with mess for a change. I'll be that crazed emperor who fiddled while Rome burned.

"Jenny, I know you're upset, but maybe this is not the time to talk."

Gloria nods toward the kitchen as if I'm completely unaware that a two-timing man is on the premises. Of course, I could be a bit quick on the judgment trigger. After all, the only proof I have is a pink note. Maybe she's just trying to lure him away from me. Maybe he's done nothing.

So far.

My Machiavellian wheels are turning. I know I don't appear to be the kind of woman who has a thought in her head besides how to get dust bunnies from under the sofa, but I have a library card. I know my way around a good bookstore.

During the years I think of as kitchen/family focused, I've kept my mind agile with books on everything from Zen Buddhism to Native American history. Pity I didn't do the same thing with my body, but we won't go there.

I didn't read *The Art of War* for nothing. I know that if I'm to beat this insatiable wench, I've got to fight like a man.

Of course, that includes the art of the surprise attack.

"Okay, you're right, Gloria. But the minute Rick gets out of my kitchen, we've got plans to make."

I can't live on dreams of the past forever. If I want to have a future, I'd better get off my complacent butt and grab it.

CHAPTER 5

Can a woman twice dumped and lost at sea give goddess lessons?

—Gloria

Waiting on the porch with Jenny feels like sitting in the middle row at the theater waiting for the pivotal moment in the film. Your fists are balled and you're holding your breath knowing that in the next few minutes you'll expel it in a big wave of understanding. So, that's the big secret. So, he's the one who stole the million dollars. So, *she's* the mistress.

"Jenny." Rick strides onto the front porch.

She jumps as if she's been electrocuted. As her husband walks toward her I see such a mixture of love and pain and longing on her face, I want to weep.

Nothing in this world is easy. Before I met

Jenny and Rick, I used to walk into my empty house and think, if only I had someone to greet me at the door, I'd be happy. If only I had someone to put his arms around me and say, "There, there. Rest now, Gloria. You've had a hard day. Let me kiss you and make it all better."

I never dreamed that if I had someone I might walk through the door and feel anything except cherished. I never imagined I might want to tie my lover to a stake and set him on fire.

And yet, in spite of all that, Jenny loves Rick. It's as clear to me as if she had it stamped across her forehead.

"There's no major damage in the kitchen," Rick says. "I think I got most of the soot off the walls."

"Good."

Rick sags and Jenny stiffens while they stare at each other like gladiators facing a fight to the death.

"Jenny, I brought lunch from the restaurant."

"I thought you just came for the pies."

"Let me get the food." He hurries toward his Jeep and comes back with two take-out boxes which he places in Jenny's lap. "It's meat loaf. We had meat loaf and baked chicken on the lunch buffet today."

"You're not staying?"

"I have lots to take care of."

After he drives off, Jenny says, "I'll just bet."

Then she tells me about the pink note, the late nights at the restaurant, the unused marriage bed, even the fights over Angie. Hearing her is like watching the American dream unravel.

Still, in spite of seeing the downside of marriage firsthand, I can't give up on the notion that I've been cheated, that there's a richness and depth to life I've never experienced except vicariously, as Jillian Rockwell on a daytime soap.

"Gloria, I don't know what to do anymore."

That's my cue to say something wise, to fix everything in her life with one pithy statement.

But I never could think on an empty stomach. Stress makes me hungry. I used to keep Hershey Kisses everywhere on the set so when the camera wasn't on me I could grab a bite of comfort and assurance. *Of course, my hair doesn't look like a buzzard's butt. Of course, I can act like I enjoy kissing Brandon Wallace, that horse's ass who said I had the talent of a turnip. Of course, my contract will be renewed.*

Even chocolate couldn't ensure that.

The meat loaf smells delicious and I eye the boxes with longing.

"Oh. I'm sorry." Jenny hands a box to me and I attack the food with a plastic fork, as if I haven't seen sustenance in eight days.

If my ankle doesn't hurry up and get well so I can get on a treadmill, I'm going to be the size of a truck.

"Jenny, I don't know the first thing about love and marriage. But if I were you, I'd ask him about the note."

"Good grief. He'd act as though I'd accused him of robbing banks and stealing small dogs."

"I don't mean ask if he has another woman. Just hand him the note you found and say, I don't believe I know Sylvia."

"I'd scratch his eyes out. No, I'm going to sneak down to the restaurant and spy on him."

"What are you going to do if you catch him cheating? And what if he's innocent and he catches you spying? Either way he's on the defensive. It's a script ready-made for a nasty showdown."

Jenny looks so forlorn I'm sorry I said anything. Leaning over, I reach for her hand. "What do you want, Jenny? If your life were a movie, how would you write the ending?"

"With Rick and me living happily ever after. No matter what."

"All right then. Let's fight with every weapon in your feminine arsenal. Be a bombshell. Vamp him. Bewitch him. Make him forget he ever saw that other woman. If there is another woman."

"Don't be ridiculous. I look more like an eggshell than a bombshell. And I couldn't vamp my way out of a paper bag, much less into Rick Miller's bed."

"My track record is horrible in that department, too, but Jillian Rockwell's is not. They don't call her TV's sex goddess for nothing. I'll give you lessons."

If I go from woman-who-organizes-church-picnics to talk-of-the-town, will my husband notice?

—Jenny

I CAN'T BELIEVE this. Here I am on my own front porch with none other than Jillian Rockwell, learning the secret goddess code.

After Gloria said she'd give me the first lesson in seduction, suddenly she became Jillian.

Don't ask me how. She didn't change clothes, add makeup and jewelry or even fix her hair. She didn't do a thing except close her eyes for a minute. When she looked up she was Jillian. The tilt of her head. The mysterious air. The mesmerizing eyes.

"Men love to be touched," she's saying, except it's not Gloria's ordinary husky voice; it's Jillian's sexy purr.

"You mean, hugging?"

"Hugging is nice, but I'm talking about touching your man in subtle, sensual ways."

"I don't have the foggiest idea what you're talking about." More than twenty years of diapers, teenaged diatribes and dog hair on the sofa have beaten the sensuality right out of me. Or maybe I never had any in the first place.

"I'll show you. Pretend you're Rick, and I'm you."

Gloria aka Jillian slithers my way saying, "Hello, darling."

How she can slither on a crutch is a pure miracle. And how she can capture your attention is another. I swear, if a tornado swept through my yard and uprooted every tree I still wouldn't notice a thing except her.

I nearly jump out of my pants when she caresses my cheek and briefly brushes her fingers through my hair. *I'm Rick, I'm Rick,* I keep telling myself.

What I am is too ridiculous for words.

"Did you have a nice day?" When Gloria aka Jillian drops her hand lightly onto the top of my leg, I hold my breath and wonder what in the world I'm going to do now. Sure, she's said she wants to be my friend. And sure, I asked for her help. But, lord have mercy, I never expected to be caught up in an X-rated position in broad daylight on my own front porch. I just hope that old nosey biddy from next door is not watching.

Suddenly Gloria laughs. "Relax. We're just acting."

"How'd you know I wasn't?"

"If you'd held your breath much longer, I was going to have to do CPR."

"I can tell you one thing. If you did that to Rick, he'd about have a heart attack."

"When *you* do that to Rick, he won't notice a person in the room except you."

"I thought this goddess thing was some big secret. You make it sound so simple."

"It isn't, of course. Obviously, the relationship between a man and a woman is extraordinarily complicated. But I think being feminine and sensual is a wonderful way to keep the fires of passion burning."

"I can't even get a spark. I wish I could be more like you."

"Every day for the last twenty years, I've walked into the studio and become a femme fatale. It's second nature. I can turn it on and off like a faucet."

"Why didn't you turn it on for Matt Tucker? You'd have had him on his knees proposing."

She plops back into a chair, Gloria now instead of Jillian Rockwell.

"It feels too much like acting. I'm a straightforward woman. In real life I don't want pretense. I want truth."

"My sentiments, exactly," Tuck says.

He's standing in my front yard as big as sin and twice as appealing. He and Gloria are eyeing each other as if they've spotted something good to eat, while I'm turning red as a beet. I'd die of mortification if he saw the little seduction lesson. Of course, I know he's not one to eavesdrop, but who wouldn't want to watch Gloria when she goes into action?

Tuck gives me this great big smile, and from the ways his eyes are sparkling I'd bet my bottom dollar that he's now privy to the code.

"Thanks to Jackson, nobody hears my car. That boy's a genius with machines."

It's a black Jag, well-suited to him. Tuck's like a big cat, all muscle and grace, stealth and cunning. I mean this in the best of ways, of course.

He has one booted foot propped on my front-porch step, and belatedly I remember my manners.

"Have a seat, Tuck."

When he tells me he was passing through and dropped by to discuss plans for the benefit, I know he's making up excuses. Tuck never drops by. He consults his daily planner and writes down appointments and keeps them to a T. I've served on enough boards with him to watch him in action.

His unprecedented departure from the rules makes me want to stand on my front porch and announce to the whole world, *See. Love is out there if you just know how to reach out and grab it.*

"I hope you don't mind that I didn't call first." He's talking to me. He's even looking at me, but he's hardly even aware I'm on the porch. I can almost see his pheromones leaping toward Gloria. If she were vanilla ice cream, he'd be eating her with a spoon.

"Of course not. You're always welcome here."

And oh my gosh. Look at her. Reclining in that chair in her goddess persona, her eyes at a sultry half-mast, her right hand lightly caressing her left arm. I feel like I'm watching a love scene with Elizabeth Taylor and Richard Burton. *Antony and Cleopatra*.

I wonder if she's even aware of what she's doing, of the effect she's having on him.

Gloria hasn't said a word, but the way Tuck's attention is riveted on her, you'd think he was the United Nations and she was unveiling a sure-fire plan for world peace.

"Jenny and I are co-chairs for the benefit for the Volunteer Fire Department."

This is so thrilling, to see romance abloom on my own front porch.

"I have a wonderful idea," I tell them. "Wouldn't it be great if we could advertise that

Gloria will be at the benefit, signing autographs? We'd get a ton of people." I turn to her. "Gloria, would you?"

"If it would help you, Jenny, I'd be happy to."

"Great. Why don't I get some sweet tea while you two discuss it?"

I practically float into the kitchen. The only thing better than having a great relationship yourself is being the instigator in somebody else's good time.

Maybe if I dawdle long enough, Gloria and Tuck will…oh, I don't know. Kiss? That's a bit premature. I'd be happy if I could walk onto my front porch and see him reach over to touch her hand.

Or vice versa. If Gloria leaves her alter ego Jillian in the driver's seat, there's no telling what will happen.

I swipe at a few smoke stains on the wall, then spot my roses lying on the floor, neglected. I'll fix a tray, add a few cookies from the cookie jar and the Gertrude Jekyll roses.

When I get my favorite crystal vase, I remember the day Rick and I bought it at a yard sale. The old couple who sold it said it had been a wedding gift to them, and through the years they'd filled the vase with roses on every special occasion—birthdays, holidays, anniversaries.

They had no children and were selling their possessions because she had to go to an assisted living home, and he was going with her. They held hands the entire time, and looked at each other with such joy and tender regard I knew it was possible to love someone so dearly you couldn't bear to be without them. Ever.

On the drive home, Rick and I talked about the couple. He swore we would be like that, and I believed him.

Gathering the drooping roses, I spot Rick's jeans, and the romantic steam hisses right out of me.

How easy it is to make promises and how hard to keep them.

All the wilting roses need is a bit of water and they'll perk right back up. If only it were as easy to revive a wilting marriage.

Just add water and voila, Rick and Jenny Miller kiss and make up, then life becomes a Currier and Ives Christmas print, everybody smiling and holding hands while peace and joy reign forever.

Maybe I'm just old-fashioned, focusing so hard on Rick and marriage I've neglected to take stock of myself. I wonder what would happen if I got in my truck and drove off somewhere to find the real me.

CHAPTER 6

How do you tell if a hero is real or make-believe?

—Gloria

While I wait for Jenny, I ask Tuck about the benefit. He tells me it's a barbecue picnic, and practically everybody in Mooreville and the surrounding communities will be there. The annual event is always on his farm and he donates the barbecue.

I make some inane comment—"How nice of you"—then sit back, watchful. The Matt Tucker on Jenny's front porch is likeable and approachable, not at all like the big arrogant male I'd met astride his black stallion.

"I guess you know I didn't drop by to discuss a barbecue with Jenny." His smile is boyish, slightly lopsided and extraordinarily charming.

"No, I don't know that. I don't walk on water, in spite of what my fans think."

"I'm shy, Miss Hart."

"Call me Gloria."

"Most people mistake it for arrogance. If I seemed that way at Jack's garage, I just came by to apologize."

I'm amazed. In the space of five minutes Matt Tucker has turned into somebody I'm thinking couldn't be more perfect if I'd put in my order with God. Listen, I know all this sounds mystical and shallow and immature, but I've been paired with some of Hollywood's most handsome, richest, most sought-after leading men. Who you fall for is not about looks and desirable assets. It's not even about character and matching interests, though heaven knows, those qualities ought to count.

In the end, perfect matches are about spirit and soul and passion. They are about magic.

Though that sort of connection has eluded me, in my heart I know it exists.

"Gloria?" As Tuck leans toward me, I notice that his eyes are green with warm starbursts in the middle. "How long will be you here?"

"Until Jackson gets my Ferrari fixed. At least a week, probably."

"And you'll go back to resume your career?"

"I'm not sure."

What happened to going back to Hollywood to kick some serious butt? Where's the career-oriented, totally focused Gloria who never lets anything get the best of her, who is determined to convince the producers that America's soap-opera fans can't live without her?

Obviously, Jillian has taken over my body—which is leaning dangerously close to Tuck—and she's intent on taking over my life, reshaping it to suit her own needs. The thing is, being Jillian feels right. She knows how to let herself fall into a moment, how to let every one of her feelings show, how to balance her personal life with her career as investigative reporter.

Of course, I'm not Jillian, not really, and this is Mooreville, Mississippi, not *Love in the Fast Lane*.

Or is it? Tuck and I are now listing toward each other like two clipper ships, sails billowing and the winds of Fate carrying us at will.

"It depends," I add in Jillian's breathless purr. It has been the undoing of more than one Tinsel-Town hunk and it seems to be working on Mooreville's answer to Hollywood's A-list of leading men. Not that I'm trying to vamp. I'm just letting myself ride this tidal wave of raw emotion.

"On what?"

"I don't know. Things."

I catch a glimpse of chest hair above the top of a white shirt. Dark, tipped with gold.

Jillian runs her tongue around her lips and so do I. This man is delicious. And I want a taste. Just one. Then I'll go back to the west coast happy.

He leans closer, touches my arm, runs his fingertips from elbow to wrist then briefly squeezes my hand. And it's better than any kiss I've ever had, more satisfying, more real.

"If there's anything I can do for you, let me know."

Put your hand back, I want to tell him. Make me feel that way again. Make me feel as if I've never been touched until your hand made contact with my skin. As if I'm the only woman in the universe, and you're the only man.

I've come undone.

"Anyone ready for tea and cookies?"

Jenny's standing in the doorway, too bright-faced and perky, a cat-who-swallowed-the-cream look on her face. She saw, she knows. And she's tickled.

"Thanks, but I have to be going."

After he leaves, Jenny sits in the rocking chair and hands me a glass of tea.

"That went well," she says.

"I don't know."

"Of course it did. My gosh, he was touching you just like you showed me." She takes a guilty bite of cookie. "I didn't mean to be spying. Really. I just happened to be in the doorway."

"Jenny, I'm a great big fraud. I owe you an apology."

"For what?"

"What I don't know about men would fill an encyclopedia. Maybe two. I didn't know what in the world I was talking about when I gave you that so-called seduction lesson."

"Does anybody ever know the opposite sex? Even one you've lived with for twenty-three years?"

Never comfortable in uncertain waters, I change the subject to the benefit, tell Jenny I need to use her phone. I need to arrange to have the studio head send publicity photographs to sign at the barbecue. I need to check my messages.

Most of all, what I need is to find my footing, ground myself in familiar territory and move forward. Focused. In charge.

Unbidden, the memory of Tuck's touch waylays me, and I stare over the top of my sweet tea wondering if it's possible to have it all.

WE GO BACK inside where Jenny calls the press about my involvement in the benefit. Then I call home to listen to my telephone messages while she's doing something else—laundry, I think.

"Gloria Hart, where in tarnation are you? Gone to hell in a handbasket without me, more than likely."

Roberta's third message, screamed loudly enough to break the sound barrier, jerks me back to my real self, the self who can't make up her mind what she wants nor how to get it.

"If you don't return this call, I'm sending a posse after you. Much as I hate to admit it, I'm worried about you. You've probably gone off and got your skinny butt in trouble." If only Roberta knew. "And I know you can't get out without me. You don't know up from Adam."

She's got that right. I dial Roberta's cell phone and tell her about the accident.

"And you did all this when?" She shouts. "And I'm just now finding out? I ought to hop on a plane for the specific purpose of giving you a piece of my mind."

"You do that every day, Roberta. Why don't I just pull one of your lectures out of my memory and make do with that?"

"Don't you get sassy with me. You forget who you're talking to. I don't get mad, I get even."

From the way we talk, you'd think we don't like each other, but just the opposite is true. Sometimes I think our constant sparring is the only way I can tell I'm connected to the real world. I can't say the same for Roberta. She's like a World War II army tank. She knows exactly where she stands and she rules the ground she stands on. Nothing stops her.

"How's the vacation, Roberta?"

"If I never see another beach it'll be all right with me. I look like a shriveled up old frog and I won't even begin to describe Hubert."

Hubert's her husband of forty years, and, in spite of the way she talks about him, Roberta loves him fiercely.

"They can have Puerto Vallarta for all I care," she says.

"I thought you were in Cancun."

"Wherever. All I know is I'm tired of being someplace where nobody speaks my language. How come you left without letting me know? Are you in some kind of trouble you're not telling?"

I tell her that Jillian's private plane went down over the Atlantic.

"Currently I'm lost at sea."

"In a nutshell, you got canned. And you want me to think up a way to rescue you."

"Yes. You're good at scheming."

"Does anything go?"

"As long as it's legal."

"That lets out my best plan. Murder. I've been wanting to coat that producer with peanut butter and hang him out for the buzzards ever since he killed off Dirk." My fictional husband, and the only man who ever made Roberta wish she was a tramp. Or so she claims.

Now that Roberta's on the job, I feel confident that nothing can stop me from snatching back my limelight.

I'm on the phone to the studio about sending publicity shots when Angie walks in looking flushed and up to her ears in trouble. Now what?

Jenny already has more problems than she can handle. The last thing she needs is to have her daughter dump another load of trouble in her lap.

Angie sprawls on the sofa, her long, tanned legs stretched out for what looks like miles. "Hi, Miss Hart. What 'cha doing?"

"Call me Gloria. Please." I hang up then sit beside her and tell her about plans for the barbecue.

"Neat. All my friends will want your autograph." Twisting her long hair around her fingers, Angie shifts her gaze from me to the window.

I wonder what she's thinking, what she's dreaming. She reminds me of myself at her age—high-strung, independent, sometimes belligerent. In Angie, I see so clearly what I've missed. Sure, she's a challenge, but not having children suddenly seems like such a lonely choice.

Would it hurt if I borrow her for just a little

while? Get to know her as if she were my own? Maybe I'll be helping Jenny, too. Maybe I can take a bit of the pressure off her.

"Angie, do you have time to drive me into town? I need to replace my cell phone."

"Sure."

After I talk to Jenny, we climb into Angie's red Valiant. She peels out of the driveway and nearly mows down the Millers's mailbox. Resisting the urge to yell *stop!* then climb out of the car, I lean back and listen while Angie points out the sights—her school, her best friend's house, Jackson Tucker's garage.

Suddenly she says, "How old were you when you first had sex?"

Oh my Lord. I asked for it. Now what am I going to do? Where's a script when I need it?

"I don't remember, Angie." I know. *I know.* It's a cop-out.

"I saw that flashback episode where Jillian Rockwell did it when she was sixteen. It was so cool."

I think I hate Jillian Rockwell.

"That was fiction. A plot thread to reel in viewers."

"But you wouldn't ask anybody's permission. Right?"

I had almost forgotten the earnestness and confusion of youth, the power of peer pressure.

"Angie, I have never let anybody take something I wasn't ready to give."

She doesn't answer, and I look out the window to see which way we're going. Not that I would know. All I know is that mothering has to be the toughest job in the world.

I also know that at the rate the fence posts are whizzing by, I won't have to worry about getting my job back. I'll be lost forever in Mooreville, Mississippi. Six feet under.

If being an adult is all that complicated, they'd have remedial classes so some folks could pass.

—Angie

THE REALLY COOL thing about Miss Hart is not just that she told me to call her Gloria, but she's riding with me without white-knuckling the door handle.

The other really cool thing is that she doesn't lecture like you-know-who.

And here's another thing: she's treating me

like an adult, like I have more than two brain cells in my head.

She's great looking, too. Not like Mom, who wears stuff that looks like it came over on the Mayflower.

Listen, if I let myself go like that when I'm old and thirty, just throw me in the lake.

If love is a mountain, how did I end up on an anthill?

—Jenny

WELL, here I am in my own bedroom after the longest day of my life. Rick's bent over taking off his socks and I'm thinking this is not the night to employ the tactics I learned from Jillian Rockwell.

Timing is everything. Or so I've read. Somehow seduction and nearly burning the house down don't go together.

"Angie took Gloria to get a new cell phone this afternoon," I say.

"Good. She seems to feel better today."

"Gloria?"

"Yeah, who'd you think I meant?" He pads to the bathroom in bare feet and I wait till the toilet flushes before I tell him about Angie peeling out of our driveway this morning like it was the Talledega Speedway.

"Why don't you lay off her, Jenny?"

Great. I've started another fight.

"You always take up for her, Rick."

"She's a good kid. You just need to trust her."

He's standing in the doorway stark-naked, and if he had any idea of planting the flag, he forgot about bringing along the pole.

Problems with Angie pale beside my sudden rage. I want to throw the pink note in his face, then slap him till his ears ring. I want to yell *How could you? What do you mean spending your time with a pink-lipped trollop while I'm in the kitchen making your infernal pies?*

The only thing that saves me is Gloria in the spare bedroom. Not Gloria, the Hollywood star, but Gloria, my friend who came back from the ride with my daughter looking pale and tired.

I make a mental note to insist that she rest tomorrow. A second not to burn the pies. A third not to rile Rick about Angie. Another not to dwell on the mystery woman writing pink notes to my husband. To forget about matchmaking and tend to my own shaky relationship.

My list is about a mile long. Which just goes to prove my life's a complete mess.

I wish Rick would put on some clothes. It ought to be against the law for a man that age to look that good naked.

CHAPTER 7

Oh, Romeo, wherefore art thou, and why do I need a baseball bat instead of a ladder?

—Gloria

The sound of something pelting against the outside bedroom wall shatters my dreams and sends me scurrying to the window.

Shades of Romeo and Juliet! Tuck is standing in the shadow of Jenny's giant magnolia tree looking mysterious and romantic, and he's motioning for me to come outside.

There's probably a rule somewhere about trysts in the moonlight when you're a guest in Mooreville, Mississippi, but I've always been a rule-breaker. Grabbing my outrageously vampish red silk robe and my relentlessly awkward crutch, I sneak through the darkened house and hurry outside. I feel sixteen.

"Gloria. Over here."

"Oh my lord, *Jackson* Tucker."

"Yeah. It's me. I had to see you."

"At one o'clock in the morning? Are you crazy?"

"Maybe I am."

He starts to lift his hand, and all of a sudden I see myself dragged off by the hair in the middle of the night, headlines screaming, TV's Goddess Abducted by Mooreville's Mechanic: Raging Hormones on Both Sides Blamed.

I swing the crutch upward toward his more sensitive body parts, and we both topple and land in an ignoble heap.

"That hurt." He should complain. I have him by quarter of a century. Frightful thought.

While he's rolling around clutching his groin, I roll the other way trying to get my old, bruised knees untangled and working. Jackson grabs the hem of my robe.

"What did you think I was going to do? Maul you?"

"I thought you were going to grab me."

"I was brushing my hair out of my eyes. Honest. I just wanted to talk. That's all."

"And you couldn't wait till morning?"

"It was a spur-of-the-moment thing. I didn't notice what time it was."

"It's time for old ladies to be in bed and bad boys to go home."

If anybody but me had called me an old lady, I'd cut out his tongue.

What would Matt Tucker think if he knew I was rolling around in the dirt with his son? And what if something develops between Matt and me? Something serious? I could end up Jackson Tucker's stepmother.

Somebody in this Universe must have a warped sense of humor.

Jackson helps me up, all gentleman now but still, little more than a kid.

"Angie said she talked to you, that you were real nice."

"She's not pregnant, is she?"

"No. We use protection."

I'm not sure I wanted to know that. And I'm not sure I should be standing in the heady sweetness of Jenny Miller's magnolia tree at oh-lord o'clock discussing something that is clearly none of my business. Especially with a young man whose father is the object of my lustful dreams.

It's just that I've never had a really close friend except Roberta, and that's different because she's also my employee. I don't know where the lines are drawn regarding family secrets and helping somebody versus meddling.

A quick sideways glimpse of Jackson, and he could be his daddy, and all of a sudden I don't know anything anymore.

Clearly I've become unhinged by magnolias.

"Go home," I tell him. "Don't ever do this to me again. We'll talk later. In broad daylight."

I hurry toward the house not caring a whit about my exit but caring deeply that I don't inadvertently do anything to hurt this little family. I know, I know. As Roberta would say, "I'm not going to know you, girl, if you turn into a nice person."

Besides, *nice* is not what it's going to take to fight for my TV role.

I sneak back into my bed and pull the covers over my head and hope I sleep.

I also send a prayer into the Universe that I don't metamorphose into Miss Goody Two-Shoes. Survival in my business requires guts and moxie.

"Just spare me a claw or two. Please."

Holy shit, and why do I keep stepping in it?

—Jenny

"HOLY shit!"

Of all the ways I want to be roused from sleep, hearing my husband's outraged bellow is not one of them. Opening one eye, I lean on my elbow and sneak a peek at the clock. Five-thirty.

The front door rattles and Rick yells, "Jenny. Open this door."

Now what? He's going to wake the whole neighborhood.

Hurrying in bare feet, I fling open the front door and there is my husband, caught in the cross beams of flashbulbs. In his shorts. Holding the newspaper in front of his crotch.

"Oh...my...gosh."

He streaks through and slams the door, then leans against it looking wild-eyed.

"Jenny, where did all those people come from?"

"Why didn't you just come back inside?"

"I locked myself out. And you didn't answer my question."

"They're reporters."

"And they're here at the crack of dawn because..."

"I called the media?"

"Another of your benefits."

He says *benefits* the way you'd say *armed robbery*.

"You needn't act like somebody's poked a gun in your back. It's for the Volunteer Fire Department."

I add that last praying it will help. Judging by his stiff, self-righteous stance, I can see it didn't. But does that stop me? Oh, no. I plow forward, digging my own grave.

"Gloria's going to sign autographs. Tuck thinks it's a good idea. And I'd think you would, too."

He heads to the bedroom and I continue talking to his back. "I said, I'd think you would, too, since you're so all-fired busy putting out everybody else's fire you can't even put out your wife's."

There's blistering silence from our bedroom, and thank goodness all's quiet from Angie's and Gloria's rooms too.

But not the front door. The press is out there knocking like I'm the third little pig and they're fixing to blow my house down.

Speaking of which...Rick whizzes by so fast I'm nearly sucked under by his tailwinds.

"Rick!" He's out the back door before I can say diddly-squat.

Dressed, might I add. Thank goodness.

The knock sounds again and I jerk open the door.

"What?"

"Mrs. Miller, what's it like to have the goddess of daytime TV in your house?"

Great. Here's another situation I've created, even if I didn't do it on purpose. If I don't do something about it, every petunia I have is going to be tromped into the ground. Even worse, my husband is going to be front-page news in his tighty-whities.

"If you'll wait there until I change clothes and if you promise not to run pictures of my husband nearly naked, I'll come out and answer your questions. Deal?"

"Deal."

Lord, I just hope they keep their promise.

BY THE TIME the reporters leave and I've flopped down at the kitchen table to catch my breath with a cup of coffee, the phone rings.

"I heard about the commotion at Rick's house."

Godzilla never says hello and she never acknowledges that I'm part of Rick's life in any way, fashion or form. She even calls Angie Rick's child.

Years ago, I gave up trying to please her. Believe me, if I had caller ID in the kitchen, I'd never have picked up the phone.

"Good morning to you, too, Lulu."

"If I'd caused the ruckus you did this morning, I wouldn't be acting so smarty-pants about it."

Usually I'll do just about anything to keep the peace with my mother-in-law, but I'm already so far in the doghouse, I'm feeling reckless.

Maybe a bit liberated, too. Maybe Gloria's spunk and Jillian's goddess persona are rubbing off on me.

In a situation like this I think the goddess code needs an addendum: add arrows, pull string, smile.

"I see the neighborhood grapevine is working overtime."

"I can talk to anybody I please."

And I know who that *anybody* is. Sometimes I think my neighbor Patty Jones does nothing except watch my house with her spyglasses for the express purpose of calling Lulu to report my every move.

"You caught me redhanded, Lulu. I'm a smarty-pants. A troublemaker, too. Let's see?

What else can we add? Oh, I know. Terrible wife and worse daughter-in-law."

She hangs up. Great. She'll call Rick and repeat the conversation word for word and I can add another nail to the doghouse I'm in. Suddenly, I come undone.

"Jenny?" I didn't hear Gloria come in. She's standing in the doorway giving me funny looks. "Are you laughing or crying?"

"Both, I guess."

I tell her about my morning's escapades.

"It's all my fault. I should have warned you the reporters would invade. I'm sorry."

"I'm not. This is the best publicity our benefit has ever had. Besides, I haven't seen my husband move that fast since he chased me around the play gym set when we were chubby children."

"This calls for girlfriend therapy. And celebration. My ankle is almost healed." Gloria does a cautious pirouette without her crutch. "A day at the spa. My treat. Is there a good one around here?"

"In Tupelo. What about Angie? And the pies?"

"Angie can come, too. And we'll pick up pies at the bakery, then deliver them to Rick. My treat."

"Can we add a little arsenic to his piece?"

"The seduction didn't work out?"

"I don't think those techniques work on grizzly bears."

"We'll just have to think of a way to revert him to teddy bear."

I feel better already.

My family ought to be on Oprah.

—Angie

DOES Mom think I don't have ears? Does she think I can't see what's going on in my very own house?

I heard that ruckus with the reporters this morning. And when I went to the kitchen to get some cereal I heard her crying. Fortunately she didn't see me, so I just backed out and pretended I hadn't heard a thing. Went back to my room and shut the door.

Not that I don't care. I mean, who wouldn't? This is my home, too, which some people I won't mention seem to forget. But does anybody ever ask my opinion? Does anybody ask how I'd feel about anything? Like divorce.

I don't even want to think about it. Instead I'm sitting here eating the cheese snacks I had stashed. If I hadn't, the way Mom's making the kitchen enemy territory, I'd starve to death.

Listen, I'm no child, in spite of what you-know-who thinks. I realize marriage is not always an old TV rerun of *The Partridge Family*. But all in all, I thought Mom and Dad had it better than most.

Boy, was I wrong. And to think, I used to aspire to be exactly like them.

"Angie?"

It's Mom. She'll have a conniption if she sees me eating junk food instead of healthy food. I stuff the cheese snacks under my pillow, swallow my last bite whole and wipe my mouth before I yell, "Come in."

She's all smiles. Like that fools me for a minute.

"How would you like to go to the spa?"

When has she ever gone to the spa? Is this a joke? A bribe?

"You're kidding. Right?"

"No. Gloria's invited us."

I should have known. At least somebody in this house thinks I'm not a little kid. But I'm not fixing to make a big deal of it.

"Sure."

Wait till I tell Sally.

Where's the script when you need it?

—Gloria

THERE'S NOTHING like being wrapped in seaweed to make a woman feel pampered.

On the tables next to me, Angie is catching a catnap and Jenny is making little humming sounds of contentment. I feel good all over just knowing I'm responsible for this few hours of pleasure. Finally I've done something to pay her back for her generosity.

After we finish our spa visit, we have a quick cup of coffee with Jenny's friend Laurel at the library, then pick up pies at Kroger's Bakery and head back to Mooreville. This is my first opportunity to see Rick's restaurant. It's rustic and homey, filled with the aroma of Southern cooking and diners who are probably friends and neighbors, most of them in jeans and baseball caps, a few wearing straw fedoras against the intense summer heat.

We've surprised Rick with the pies. He seems genuinely touched. Watching the two of them exchange guarded, almost shy looks, I can't help but believe their love is solid. If the marriage is shaky it's only because they've lost their way from each other. Now pride is in the way. And maybe complacency. Long-practiced habits of tending to business and not tending to each other.

Okay, maybe this is just Jillian Rockwell talking, but *she* knows that goddesses pay attention. Goddesses know you can't take somebody else for granted. And you for darned sure can't let them take *you* for granted.

I'm not talking about demanding expensive diamonds here. I'm talking about the important stuff, letting the one you love know you hold him in deep and tender regard. Not just on birthdays and anniversaries. Every day.

Unfortunately, I have no firsthand knowledge that my theory is correct because Jillian is the figment of a screenwriter's imagination. But I would surely like to find out.

Suddenly Tuck comes through the front door, and I'm thinking that nothing in this world is coincidence.

When he spots me, I feel a little rush at the way his eyes crinkle at the corners. Not a smile, really, not a major display of joy, just a glad-to-see-you look. And it's enough.

Rick claps Tuck on the shoulder. "Coffee's coming right up."

"Do you have time to join me, Rick? Ladies?" Tuck swings around to include Jenny, Angie and me.

It's a good thing Rick says, "I'll take the time," because I'm scared if I open my mouth I'll shout, Goody!

Rick puts his arm around his wife's waist. "Jenny, can you stay?"

"As much as I would love to, I have to call about two dozen people to organize a cakewalk for the Bougefala Baptist Church, and then I have to start putting together a roster for the diabetes telethon."

"Maybe I can help you," I tell her.

"I've got it covered. You stay and have coffee with Rick and Tuck. Angie can help me." Angie rolls her eyes, but when her daddy winks at her, she doesn't protest. "Rick can bring you home, or call my cell and I'll come and get you."

"I'll take her home," Tuck says, and I think I hear the word *eventually* tacked to the end. At least, I hope that's what I hear.

The view from our table by the window is not

much—a parking lot and a couple of oak trees looking worn-out from the heat—but there's a feeling of comfort here, of home. I can see how people settle into small towns and stay.

As we slide into our seats Tuck comments about my lack of crutch and I tell him the sprain was on my lower ankle, the crutch was just a precautionary measure for a day or two.

"Good." The way he says this, surveying me as if I'm a feisty thoroughbred he's thinking of buying, he's not talking about the condition of my ankle.

An older couple appears hard on Tuck's heels, the man in overalls, the woman in a print dress and tennis shoes. The man starts telling Tuck they're looking forward to the barbecue at his place.

He introduces them to me as Lanford and Elaine, and when she hears my name she lets out a little screech.

"My goodness. You're Jillian Rockwell." She tugs her husband's sleeve. "This is the woman I watch on TV. Quick, give me something to sign. I've got to have her autograph."

"Heck, Elaine, I don't have anything except my checkbook."

"You can have this." Rick hands me the menu, and while I sign I'm aware that Tuck is studying me with a quiet intensity.

Elaine thanks me profusely and probably would have stayed the rest of the afternoon pumping me for information about *Love in the Fast Lane*, but Rick stands and gently steers them toward the door, talking about Lanford's soybean crop as they go.

"Do you want to leave?" Tuck asks me.

"I'm used to fans. Most of them are extremely nice. The trick is to keep my feet on the ground and be who I am."

"Who are you?"

"Not Jillian Rockwell. That much I know."

"Why not?"

No one has ever asked that question. And judging by the serious way he said it, Tuck's not asking out of idle curiosity.

"Jillian's far more complicated and sophisticated than I. She's also very high-maintenance."

He glances at my emerald. "I believe you were driving a Ferrari Spyder."

"I believe you were driving a Jag. And riding a million-dollar thoroughbred stallion."

He laughs. "If I'm going to make a fool of myself, I'd prefer to do it in the privacy of my own turf. Would you like to see Tuck's Farms?"

The name turns out to be a misnomer. There's no farm-like modesty to this place. A long driveway winds through massive oaks and ancient magnolias to a house that resembles Tara in *Gone With the Wind*. Huge barns and paddocks sprawl on the west side where sleek, beautiful horses race around with their tails streaming behind like flags.

"This place could be addictive," I tell him.

"It is. I'll show you the patio where we'll be holding the barbecue. Or do you want to see the horses?"

"Horses."

There's something about a barn that's just ready-made for racing pulse and pheromones gone wild. Tuck says, "Watch your step," and puts his arm around me, then doesn't let go, even when he starts introducing me to the thoroughbreds peering over their stalls.

"Is it okay to pet them?"

"Yes. As long as I'm with you."

Reaching toward a black beauty he calls

Tucker's Mississippi Midnight, I caress the velvety muzzle. "It's so soft."

"Yes." His hand slid up my back and into my hair. "It is."

If this were a segment on *Love in the Fast Lane*, the writers would have me turn in his arms while he leaned down to kiss me. Sunlight would filter through the open doorway and romantic music would play in the background.

Alas, a cat streaks by and startles the horse, who rears up in panic. Tuck scoops me up and out of harm's way—though I don't know how much harm I'm in since the stall door looks as if it could withstand a good hurricane.

Now. Here's where the kiss is going to come. My skin gets tight with anticipation and I stop just short of puckering up.

"We'd better get you home. I keep forgetting you had a wreck just a few days ago." Tuck's still holding me, and I swear, from the look on his face you'd think he couldn't decide if I'm angel or demon.

"Well. I'm not broken." I murmur this in a noncommittal way. Jillian at work, no doubt.

"I can see that." Matt sets me down, anyway,

his eyes sparkling with amusement. "In fact, I imagine it would take something along the lines of Armageddon to break you. Are you ready?"

"At the risk of being mistaken for an outright flirt, I can tell you unequivocally that I'm always ready. For anything."

"Lord, help us all."

Roaring with laughter, he offers his arm. Obviously to keep me from tripping over heaven knows what on the way to the car, because he's making sure that not one other tiny portion of his body touches mine.

I almost wish I'd fall. I have an absurd desire to land in a pile of hay with this man.

CHAPTER 8

They give wings for things like this, but I think you have to be dead to be an angel. Or at least somebody who has never used a four-letter word.

—Gloria

Back home, Jenny looks up from the telephone and asks, "How did it go?"

"On a scale of one to ten?" I ask, and she nods, grinning. "Ten for me. Two for him. Maybe."

"Even men like Tuck run scared after a really bad marriage. Give him time. He's bound to see you're nothing like his wife."

"Maybe they should have X-rayed my head when I crashed into the light pole. What in the world am I thinking, anyway? I'll be leaving as soon as my car's fixed."

"You forgot the barbecue."

"I'll be there."

"So will Tuck."

"Don't get your hopes up, Jenny."

"Oh, but I do. And so should you."

Jenny personifies my favorite lines from Emily Dickinson: "Hope is the thing with feathers/That perches in the soul..." I can almost see the trail of feathers she leaves in her wake.

I wish I had her innocent belief in the basic goodness of mankind, in endless possibilities, in the capacity of the spirit to rise up every day and not merely prevail but triumph.

I believe in working hard and charging forward and fighting tooth and toenail for what you want and never giving up, *never*. Maybe that's the same as hope, only not quite as gentle as a thing with feathers perching in the soul.

"Show me what I can do to help." I sit down beside her in the kitchen where papers are spread all over the tabletop.

"Nothing. Just keep me company while I categorize this list of cakes."

"Where's Angie?"

"Off with Jackson Tucker. And Rick is doing God knows what. I swear, I'd like to run away."

"Drive back to California with me."

My impromptu invitation stuns both of us. We've only known each other a few days, and yet extraordinary circumstances have created an extraordinary bond.

"It would be a nice vacation for you. And the least I can do after all you've done for me."

"Oh, I can't. Definitely not. Angie needs me here."

"She can come, too."

I can just hear Roberta. *Are you out of your mind? How do you expect to regain your TV role if you're entertaining guests?*

The thing is, I don't feel out of my mind at all. I feel better than I've felt in a very long time. I could be turning into somebody I'd like to know better.

How can you land on your feet if you're in quicksand?

—Jenny

IT'S MIDNIGHT. Gloria's asleep, and Angie's finally back from heaven knows where with that wild buck, Jackson—thank goodness. And Rick's not home. Again.

In spite of a wonderful day at the spa and

Gloria's advice, not to mention my own instincts screaming that I've lost my last marble, I sneak out of the house.

The dogs perk up, wanting to come, but I tell them I'm taking care of business and it's their job to guard the house. It's dark as pitch out here. I forgot my flashlight, and besides, I don't think burglars use them.

Of course, I'm not a burglar. I'm just a wife on a mission. Is he or isn't he? Cheating, that is.

I navigate my yard without a problem. Even in the dark I know and love very bush, tree, nook and cranny. It's the vacant lot between my house and the restaurant that could be my Waterloo. The weeds are higher than my head and eager to tangle me up in their prickly fingers so the snakes lurking nearby can eat me alive.

I don't know how Napoleon would deal with all this, but if I so much as spot a weed move, I'll die on the spot. Nobody will ever find me. Angie will mourn and Rick will be sorry.

What am I doing out here defying death, anyway? I start to turn back, but the urge to find out what's *really* keeping Rick at the restaurant night after night is so strong I press on.

Finally I get across the vacant lot, but my target is at the end of a long downhill slope. Full of overgrown briar patches. And small gullies. And big rocks.

If I scream will Rick leave Miss Pink Passion Notes and come to my rescue?

I consider creeping down on all fours, but that would put me closer to the snakes. Instead I turn sideways and inch down like a crab.

Halfway down, a rock waylays me and I end up on my butt, scooting and crashing along at what feels like the speed of light. And screaming. Did I mention screaming?

At the bottom I startle a stray cat who yowls as if the world has come to an end.

And maybe it has.

Rick's in the doorway behind the restaurant backlit from the lamp in his office. And he's training a flashlight into the night.

"What the hell?"

Worse. He trains it on me.

"Jenny?

"Hello, Rick."

"What are you doing back here?"

"I was worried about you?"

When I'm in hot water I end every sentence as if it's a question. Rick knows this. As he heads toward me, I figure my marriage is now as good as dead. Killed by suspicion and snakes wearing pink high heels.

He helps me up, wipes the leaves and twigs off my shirt and my jeans, then just looks at me as if I'm somebody he doesn't even know. Just before I think I'm going to die of embarrassment if I don't die of a splinter in my butt first, my husband says, "Let's go home."

"Okay."

Sometimes it's these small, tender mercies that hold the fabric of a marriage together.

Moonlight in Mississippi has improved exponentially.

—Gloria

MY NAME is all over the local papers this morning. Jenny has them spread across the kitchen table where she's drinking coffee and looking as if she's lost her last friend. I pour myself a cup—so much at home with the Millers I know where the cutlery and dishes are located—then slide in beside her.

"Good morning. What's up?"

"I'm not sure you want to know."

"That bad, huh?"

"Worse." She tells me about her misguided midnight mission.

"Maybe you need a break. Reconsider coming to California with me."

"I'd have to talk to Rick. He didn't say a word when we got home last night, and he was gone before I got out of bed this morning. So I guess we're not speaking."

"Why don't I talk to Rick? I'll make our trip seem very casual. You won't have to burn bridges. It will just give you some breathing room."

"You're a saint, but I just don't know yet what I'm going to do. Of course, the trip would give Angie a chance to see something beyond Mooreville and Jackson Tucker, but I'm not sure this is the right time for me to leave."

I'm far from a saint, but what I'm about to do might qualify me. Either that, or label me certifiably insane.

"Even if you don't go, Angie could ride home with me and I could buy her a ticket to fly back."

"Are you sure? She can be a handful."

I can take this graceful way out or I can be a friend and keep the hope alive on Jenny's face.

"I'm sure."

AFTER BREAKFAST Jenny lets me borrow her truck while she's working in her rose garden. First I drive to the restaurant.

Rick is circulating with the coffeepot, greeting his customers. I don't think for a minute he's seeing another woman, and I told Jenny so before I left the house. I don't think she believes me.

He pours two cups then joins me. I issue the invitation to take Angie to California before I chicken out.

"Angie will be thrilled. It has meant so much for all of us to have you here. Especially Jenny. She's stuck in this little town." Rick shakes his head, as if all things female confuse him. "I don't know."

Seized by a sudden inspiration, I say, "Why don't the two of you visit me?" When he protests he can't leave the restaurant long enough to drive cross-country, I offer to buy tickets for them to fly out. "Just for a weekend, if that's all you can spare."

I can picture the two of them away from the daily stress of running a business and raising a teenager. I imagine them drinking margaritas beside my pool, sitting in side-by-side deck chairs and holding hands, recapturing all the old feelings that first brought them together.

I'm no romantic. I know capturing magic is impossible for couples who have not only grown far apart but have eviscerated each other with barbed tongues and wounded each other's spirits with cold silences. But Jenny and Rick are not like that. I think in the daily grind of living, they've simply lost sight of each other.

When Rick declines my invitation, I'm disappointed, but there's nothing else I can do. Really.

Except drive over to the garage to check on my car. And talk to Jackson.

I can just hear Roberta saying, *Are you out of your skinny mind? Who made you God?*

"Roberta, you old sourpuss, you won't even know me when I get home." I say this aloud, pulling up into Tucker's Garage, full of intentions to talk to Jackson about responsibility. And also full of hope that Jackson's father might come riding down the hill on his black stallion. That he might whisk me off to his big barn that smells of sweet clover hay and do all manner of delicious things to me in the haystacks.

I know, I know. I said I wasn't a romantic, but maybe this is Jillian talking. Maybe I'm turning into my TV persona. But only her better side.

I hope.

When I pull into the parking lot, Jackson looks up from the raised hood of a Ford Escort and waves.

"How's it going, Miss Hart?"

"I was going to ask you the same thing."

"The parts came." He takes me inside to show me the Ferrari which is looking almost as good as new. "I've got a few more little dents to pull out, then do the paint job, and she'll be ready."

"You've done splendid work."

He grins and says, "Thanks," then I move into the hard stuff.

"Jackson, Angie is only seventeen."

"Yeah. I know."

I'm not about to give a big speech about the consequences of unplanned pregnancy. It's not my job. Still, if I can help Jenny and her family, I'm willing to look like a meddler.

"There's a possibility she will drive back to

California with me, and if she does I think it's important she knows it's all right with you."

"Jeez. I'd give my eyeteeth to drive this baby across the country." He pats the hood of my car, then smiles, so much like his daddy I feel goosebumps on my arm. "You're cool, Miss Hart."

"Call me Gloria."

I glance up the hillside and see no sign of Tuck, then the cool Miss Hart does what she always does when life kicks her in the gut and her hopes are dashed. She gets into her borrowed truck and drives home.

It's funny how quickly I've come to regard the Millers' place as home. Funny, but wonderful.

Just a few days ago I would not have imagined a single good thing that could come of my accident. Now I see that nothing in this world is chance. Everything you do, everywhere you go, every person you meet is the Universe's way of saying, *Hey, be still, look, listen and learn.*

"You missed a call from Tuck," Jenny tells me when I walk in. "The number is on the hall table. He's coming by at seven to take you out. Unless you have other plans."

There are miracles, after all. For the first time

in my life, I don't mind that somebody else is taking charge.

"Did he say where?"

"No. Just to wear jeans."

TUCK AND I are sitting on a patchwork quilt on a hilltop overlooking his paddocks and a large lake. A picnic basket with the remains of thick roast beef sandwiches sits on the grass beside us, and we're holding two wineglasses filled with merlot.

The moon is the kind a set director might order, big and round and orange, so impossibly bright you'd think it's fake if you didn't know better.

Below, a horse as pale as moonlight drinks from the lake, then shakes her mane before she bounds off to join the others.

Tuck points all this out to me, calling their names and relating their racing history. Then he sits back and watches me.

"It's a kind of heaven, isn't it?" I tell him.

"Yes. I wanted you to see it. In the moonlight."

I love this about Tuck—that he wants to share the things he treasures most with me. That he doesn't apologize for not taking me to a fancy restaurant and some noisy place where the loud entertainment would make conversation impossible. That he chose the quiet panorama of a summer night where the water speaks of life, the stars speak of love and the moon speaks of eternity.

I can see why the news articles call him an authentic horse whisperer. If his deep, rich drawl has the same effect on horses it's having on me, then he can get them to do anything he wants simply by speaking.

As I turn to watch the play of moonlight across his face, I marvel that wonder can be found in such simple pleasures—a man, a voice and a moon.

"Thank you," I tell him.

He takes the wineglass from my hand, then kisses my palm. "You're welcome."

He draws me into his arms, and suddenly, I've found more than wonder. I've discovered passion and need and an urgency that can't be denied.

Tuck doesn't hesitate, doesn't pause to ask permission, doesn't ponder whether it's too soon. He bares me to the moonlight, then covers my pale body like a sun-warmed blanket.

I'll believe it when I see it.

—Angie

GLORIA HART just asked me to accompany her home.

Like Mom's going to let me go on a road trip to California by myself. If I get off without Mom, I'll guarantee you the world's fixing to come to a screeching halt. St. Peter can forget about blowing his trumpet. If Mom stays in Mooreville, Mississippi, and lets me go a thousand miles away, the world will just stop.

I mean that. Last summer she wouldn't even let me go to New York with the Drama Club. And she nearly died on the spot when I mentioned going to Paris with the French Club.

So you see my dilemma. When Gloria says, "I hope you'll come, Angie," I don't start packing.

"Are you sure it's okay with Mom?"

"You have her blessing."

Then there must be a catch. I'm going out there to be an indentured servant. Or there's some godawful little math and science camp she wants me to attend. I hate math and science.

Oh, I make A's in the subjects, but it's only because I study my head off.

Or even worse. She and Dad are getting a divorce and she wants me out of the way until it's all over.

"What about Dad? Is it okay with him?"

"He thought you'd like it. I invited him and your mom, too. They're not coming for the entire two weeks, but I think they might fly out for a weekend."

Gloria wouldn't lie. So now I can breathe. I can start packing. Even better, I can tell Sally.

"That sounds great. Thank you, Gloria."

As soon as she leaves I pick up the phone. "Sally, guess what?" When I tell her, you could hear her squeal all the way to the South Pacific. "You'll have to watch after Jackson for me. Promise?"

The next thing is to tell Jackson. Of course, I want to do this in person, and I don't want him to know how thrilled I am. Otherwise, he's liable to get the idea I don't care and start going out with that little twit, Nancy Wiggins. She thinks she owns the world just because she's a cheerleader.

Wait till she hears about me going to California in an Italian sports car with America's TV goddess.

Why can't love be as easy to serve as barbecue?
—Jenny

WELL, here we are at the benefit for the Volunteer Fire Department. Finally.

I'm so tied up in knots I could scream. Ever since I tried to sneak up behind Rick's restaurant and find out what was going on, he's been treating me like he was some polite stranger. It seems like four years ago instead of only four days.

To top it all off, my husband's running around acting so busy he hasn't said *boo* to me, and Tuck's so preoccupied being a perfect host he hasn't had a chance to speak to Gloria. A temporary condition, I'm sure, considering he's taken her out every night since they had that picnic on the hill.

Of course, Gloria didn't share particulars, but she didn't have to. I know a lovestruck woman when I see one.

The only person in my household who is acting normal is Angie. She's jumping up and down with excitement about going to California with Gloria.

If things get any frostier in my bedroom, I'll go, myself.

First, though, I have to serve this barbecue and keep smiling.

"May I help you?" I ask the woman who is swathed in chiffon scarves and a hat as big as Texas. I know practically everybody in Lee County, but I can't recall ever seeing her. She must be from Itawamba County. Or maybe Pontotoc.

People come from everywhere for almost any event that involves seeing Tuck's Farms. Plus, folks are lined up nearly to Tuck's barns in front of the green-and-white striped awning to see the nation's reigning TV goddess.

"I'll take the meat but now the slaw." The woman speaks in an accent I've never heard. She's definitely not from Mississippi. "It gives me indigestion. I want bread but for God's sake, leave off the beans. You don't want to hear what that does to me. Suffice it to say, I could clear this gathering."

"You're not from here."

I heap her plate with extra meat and bread, then motion for the rest of the line to go around her to the next server. Most people would, anyhow. At gatherings like this everybody understands that people often strike up lengthy conversations with long-lost friends and relatives. Sometimes even perfect strangers.

"No. I'm from New Jersey." She holds out a blue-veined hand loaded with diamonds. "Sylvia Comstock."

I say, "Jenny Miller," and she acts like I'm her favorite, long-lost niece rediscovered after a two-year bout of amnesia in the snake-infested jungles of the Amazon.

"Rick's wife?" I nod, wondering how she knows my husband. "Lulu didn't tell me you'd be here."

"Lulu, my mother-in-law?"

"Yes." Sylvia chuckles. "I see she's been keeping secrets again. Lulu and I have been friends for years. I've been in town for a few days, visiting."

I'd like to say she only keeps secrets from me, but I don't want to spoil her opinion of Lulu. So far, Sylvia's the only one of Godzilla's friends who didn't act like she had nails for breakfast followed by a cup of TNT. Strange, though, I never heard her mention anyone named Sylvia.

"Do you come often?"

"No, dear. This is my first visit in twenty-five years. I lived abroad until my husband passed away last year."

"If you're staying a while, do stop by the house for a visit. I'd like Angie to meet you."

"Unfortunately, I'm leaving early in the morning. But let me give you my number. I'm planning a surprise birthday party for Lulu in October, and your husband has promised to help get her to Trenton without arousing her suspicions."

Sylvia whips out her pen and scrawls her number on a little piece of paper. Pink. The color of love. The color of embarrassment.

This note is an exact match to the one I found in Rick's pants. If memory serves, so is the number.

"Are you all right, my dear?"

"Yeah. Bug in my eye." I'm so silly. I always cry when I'm overwhelmed with happiness.

"Yoohoo." Nothing can spoil happiness quicker than Godzilla, and she's heading this way. "There you are, Tootie. I thought I'd lost you."

Tootie? Well, no wonder I'd never heard of her.

"You couldn't lose me if you tried. Why didn't you tell me you had such a sweet daughter-in-law, Puddin'?"

"Isn't she a peach? Come on, Tootie, we've got to get you out of this sun before you have a heat-stroke."

I'll bet Godzilla aka Puddin' thinks I'm a peach—one with worms and black-spot blight.

Pulling another volunteer in to take my place, I race up the hill to tell Gloria my news.

CHAPTER 9

If life were a script, I could be prepared for the second act.

—Gloria

I'm wilting in this heat and a mosquito as big as my fist bit me on my back in a place I can't scratch, even if I wanted to. Which I definitely do not. I always keep smiling when I have an audience, especially this one.

After being out of sight all morning, Tuck is leaning against the support pole at the front of my striped tent, watching. When the last of the crowd heads down the hill to the barbecue line, he finally heads my way.

"You've attracted quite a crowd." He slides into the chair beside me, his smile easy, his body language relaxed. "And you make it look easy to handle them."

"It is. I enjoy meeting people." Kicking off my sandals, I wiggle my toes in the sweet-smelling grass. "This place makes it easy. It's very relaxing. I'll bet you spend as much time as you can in that hammock out back. And with a good book."

"Are you psychic? I just read the latest Grisham book. In my hammock."

"I'd love to try it sometime."

"One of the few places we haven't." Tuck's eyes crinkle as he hands me one of the cardboard fans spread across the table, compliments of Bougefala Baptist Church, complete with a picture of the agony in the garden.

I'm feeling a bit of agony, myself. The agony of desire. The agony of wanting something I can't have. The agony of indecision. Go or stay? California or Mississippi?

"You don't have a hammock in Hollywood?"

"I do, but I don't have this view. It's amazing."

"Then perhaps you'll stay."

"Is that an invitation?"

"Yes." He lifts my right hand, turns it over and circles his thumb on the palm. "Would you like to go inside? Out of the heat?"

"Yes." Out of the heat? No. I'm a volcano, and I want him to dive right into the hot lava.

He puts the back soon sign on the table, then slides his arm around my waist as we hurry toward his house.

"Miss Hart!"

I turn and flashbulbs explode in my face. Reporters rush forward to record Gloria Hart *en deshabille* with the famous owner and trainer of thoroughbred horses.

I'm certain that's what the headlines will say. Tuck's arm is around me, my hair is mussed up from the humidity and looks like I just tumbled out of bed, and my sandals are under the table where I ran off and left them.

The reporters start firing questions. "How did you two meet?" "Are you staying in Mississippi?" "What about your romance with your co-star in *Love in the Fast Lane?*" "Is it over?" "Mr. Tucker, how does it feel to be cozy with America's sex goddess?"

"No comment." His reply is as terse as his face. "Gloria, do you want to leave? I can get you out of here."

"I can handle this."

Tuck turns and walks away. But not before I see his face. Clearly, he's seeing me through the lens of his past: I'm a mistake he can't bear repeating.

I can handle this. Four little words. And I can never take them back.

I wonder what would have happened if I'd said, yes, take me away. I will never know.

Smiling, my stomach clenching with regret, I turn to deflect the reporters' questions.

How did Love in the Afternoon turn to One Flew Over the Cuckoo's Nest?

—Jenny

I TRIED to talk Gloria out of moving up her departure date, but after what happened with the reporters at Tuck's place this afternoon, she says there's no reason for her to linger.

She and Angie will be leaving tomorrow. While they've gone to Wal-Mart for a few travel toiletries, I'm in my daughter's room packing things I know she'll need but will go off and leave behind if I don't personally put them in her suitcase. Her hairbrush. Her toothbrush. I know you can pick these things up anywhere, but still,

I don't want Gloria to have to make umpteen stops just because Angie's careless.

Her diary. Ever since she was a little girl, Angie has always recorded the major events of her life. I pull the book out of her desk and stand there, tempted. I know it's wrong to read another person's diary, but when she's your own daughter and you're worried that she's doing no telling what, including having unprotected sex, wouldn't you sneak a peek?

"Jenny?"

Oh my gosh, Rick's home. In the middle of the afternoon. In spite of the fact that we were both at the barbecue earlier and he knows I didn't have time to make pies.

"In here."

"Hey. What're you doing?"

How'd he get to Angie's room so fast? And why do I feel guilty just because I'm still holding my daughter's diary? Which I absolutely did not intend to read.

"Just packing a few things for Angie." I toss the diary toward her suitcase, and, thank goodness, he never notices what it is. I can tell you one thing—it wouldn't have passed without comment. "What are you doing home?"

"I just thought I'd leave my assistant in charge for a while and spend some time with my family." My hopes rise up there with kites. "This is Angie's last day home."

Naturally he'd want to spend time with his daughter. I'm about to say, *It's not as if she's going to Outer Mongolia,* when my better self takes over. For once.

"I'm glad you're here," I tell him, and he says, "Yeah?"

His smile is that little crooked grin I've loved since I was thirteen and started noticing such things. But maybe it's more. Maybe it's opportunity.

Sidling up to him in what I know is nothing as hot as Jillian Rockwell's sexy slither but what I hope is a bit seductive, I put my hand on his shoulder and run my fingers down his arm.

"What do you say? Want to have some fun?"

"Where's Angie? And Gloria?"

"Gone. To Wal-Mart. And the movies. They won't be back for a while."

He puts both hands on my shoulders and walks me backward to our bedroom. This is getting good. If I were dressed in my black nightgown instead of sweaty shorts and a T-shirt, it would be even better.

Just inside the doorway I stand on tiptoe and plant one of those big, want-to-eat-you-up kisses on my husband. He tries to back me to the bed, but I want to make a big production. I want the ending to this long dry spell to be something he'll remember when we're ninety-five. I want him to look at me from our side-by-side rocking chairs in the nursing home and say, *Do you remember that day you did the striptease in the middle of the afternoon and we ended up making love on the floor? In broad daylight?*

Sidestepping, I slither out of my shorts, inventing moves I'll bet Gypsy Rose Lee never thought of. Rick swaggers toward the dresser to take off his watch, while I search behind my back for the hook to my bra. Maybe I'll fling it onto the bedpost. Maybe I'll toss it over the lampshade. Heck, the way I'm feeling, maybe I'll send it flying to the moon.

"I was wondering where this was."

My bra hits the floor with a dull thud. Rick's holding up the pink note with Sylvia's telephone number.

"I thought I'd lost it. Where'd you find it, Jenny?"

"Sylvia gave it to me? At the barbecue?"

Standing there like he's glued to the floor, it takes my smart husband all of six seconds to put two and two together.

"You found my note." This is not even a question, and I just nod my head. "And you thought I was having an affair."

I've suddenly developed a burning interest in finding out if my bra landed near my feet or over by the bed.

"And now that you've figured out I'm not cheating, you want to make love."

"All right. All right. I thought it. How could I not? You're at the restaurant all the time."

"Why would I ever come home, Jenny? You're too busy organizing the world to pay attention to anybody else. Even your own daughter."

"Leave Angie out of this."

Rick stalks to his closet and pulls down his suitcase, and I think I've died. Standing up. Rigor mortis has set in and they'll have to break my bones to get me in the casket.

"The fact is, Jenny, I'd have to tattoo Red Tag Sale on my butt to get you to notice me."

"Where are you going?" I'm still rooted to the spot, the living dead, waiting for undertakers to carry me out.

"I have some thinking to do."

"Don't go. Not on Angie's last day." Finally I find my feet. Racing over I clutch his arm. "Rick, don't go. Please.

"You're right. I misjudged you, I've been busy, I don't pay attention." I slump down onto the mattress. "But it can't be all my fault, Rick. Sometimes I feel like the only reason you have me around is to cook your infernal pies."

Rick sags down beside me, and for a while we sit there, two tired old mules trying to carry a load that has suddenly grown too heavy for us.

When he touches my knee, I think that if we can just get past this moment, we'll be all right. If we can just hold each other and say *I'm sorry, I really do trust you and in spite of what it looked like the night you caught me in the bushes behind the restaurant, I have never, ever stopped loving you*, we can move forward. Not the same. Never the same. But stronger, somehow, like seasoned oaks that survived Katrina and put down deeper roots against another storm.

He touches my knee, and I think the worst is over. But then he pulls his hand back as if I have some serious disease and might contaminate him.

"What are we going to do, Jenny girl?"

I've cheered Rick through starting his own business, fending off Godzilla's protests that he was meant for greater things, worrying about financing Angie's college education and thinning hair. I've held his hand through flu, knee-replacement surgery and dandruff.

But I've lost my megaphone and I'm fresh out of pom-poms. I don't know the answer to his latest question. If I did I'd bottle me and sell myself for a million dollars. The magic pill that fixes everything.

"I don't know," I tell my husband, and it sounds like bells tolling for a broken marriage.

CHAPTER 10

If this is freedom, why am I wearing a ball and chain?

—Angie

Naturally, I knew I'd never get off to California without Mom. The only good thing I can say is that Dad bought me a cell phone before I left, and Gloria has let me drive the Ferrari.

Talk about a high. When I tell Sally, she's going to flip. Of course, I'm not fixing to call her from the car while you-know-how is listening. Ditto, Jackson.

Fortunately Mom has a small bladder and she's been drinking lots of coffee, so we're taking plenty of rest stops. Which suits me fine.

I can call my friends and pretend everything is all right. I can pretend I didn't leave my Daddy back home by himself looking like he was shipping me to off to the New World to become a mail-order bride. He even looked sad to see Mom go.

I swear. I'll never understand adults, even if I live to be forty.

Armageddon, and that's all I'm going to say.

—Gloria

"YOU'RE doing *what?* With *who?*"

Sitting in my car in the parking lot of a truck stop on the outskirts of Las Vegas, I hold my cell phone away from my ear so Roberta's screech won't damage my hearing.

"With *whom*, Roberta."

"I don't give a rat's ears about *who* and *whom*. All I want to know is if you've lost your tiny mind?"

Roberta has a one-track mind, which is great if you want her to focus on a problem with the tenacity of a heat-seeking missile. But it's a pain in the neck if you want her to understand why you're bringing home a lovesick teenager and a heartbroken woman.

"You're going to need every ounce of energy

you can muster to make the producers eat crow for firing the goddess of daytime TV."

"I can't think about that right now, Roberta. Get over to the house and make sure everything is ready. We'll be home tomorrow."

"I didn't sign on to babysit anybody except you."

"Listen, Jenny's going through a trial separation and dealing with a daughter with raging hormones. Besides, she took care of me as if I were family. I expect you to be nice."

"You and what army are going to make me? I'm not even nice to you."

"You're all bark and no bite, Roberta. Make sure there are flowers in every room. Roses."

"I don't know how I'm going to have time for all that and keep up with your fan mail, too."

"How much mail?"

"You've got a stack in your office about the size of a small elephant, and so much spilling into mine I don't have room to turn around, let alone think."

"And?"

"Your fans are clamoring for Jillian to come back."

"Roberta, I could kiss you."

"You do, and when I get through, you'll be too marked-up to land a role as the bride of Frankenstein."

"Thanks, Roberta. I love you, too."

"Baloney."

I call my agent next, only to hear the depressing news that there is no news. I toy with the idea of calling Tuck, then quickly discard that as the rash act of a desperate woman. Instead I go inside where Jenny is sitting at a corner booth nursing a cup of coffee.

"Where's Angie?"

She nods toward the magazine rack. Her daughter's standing there, hip slung, her new cell glued to her ear.

"Talking to Jackson. For the eighty-nine-thousandth time."

"It'll be all right." I squeeze her hand. "Are you hungry?" She nods and I signal the waitress, who brings coffee and menus.

Jenny orders for Angie, too. "Maybe I should call Rick. I always do a load of towels on Monday. We're running low on coffee, and he's probably out of milk by now."

She's wadded her napkin and is now shredding

it. A piece drifts, confetti-like, toward her coffee, and when she sees it floating in her cup she gives me an astonished look.

"I'm being ridiculous."

"You're entitled."

"Thank you for not telling me to let him remember his own darned milk."

"You're welcome."

She fishes the napkin out with her coffee spoon, starts to take a drink, then changes her mind and signals the waitress for a fresh cup.

"Let him remember his own darned milk." She grins at me over the top of her cup.

Finally her spunk's showing. For the first time since we left Mississippi, I see a spark of hope for Jenny.

I wish I could say the same for me. It will take more than a flood of fan mail to convince the powers that be that *Love in the Fast Lane* will perish without Jillian Rockwell.

And I don't even want to think about Matt Tucker. After reporters stormed me at the barbecue, I saw him only once. *Thank you for helping with the benefit*, is all he said while I stood there trying to think of something witty and clever that would make him see me as he once had—not the result of studio hype, but a real woman.

In Mississippi, away from the daily grind of managing a household and a career while never letting down my guard, never letting anyone see my vulnerable side, it was easy to believe I might have it all. Easy to imagine I could regain status as TV's goddess while maintaining a sizzling cross-country relationship with a man who rings every one of my chimes.

I guess it's true you can't really leave your problems behind. The closer I get to home, the more I feel their weight descending on my shoulders. Only hours away from Hollywood, I'm shedding my famous-guest-who-has-it-all skin and becoming the aging Gloria Hart, almost has-been.

Don't count me out, though. In spite of the fact that I'm returning to a town that worships youth, I have brains and guts.

And I spit in the face of Botox.

As we leave the truck stop and approach the neon billboards of Las Vegas, Angie says, "Can we spend the night here? I've never seen a casino."

"They won't let you in," I tell her. "And I

don't think lying about your age is a very good idea, do you?"

"Absolutely not," Jenny says, but Angie just plugs in her iPod and tunes us out.

Maybe I could have been more subtle, but I think she got the point. If she's too young to gamble, she's certainly too young to settle for Jackson Tucker. No matter how good-looking he is.

No matter how much he makes me think of his daddy.

I know. I know. I'm losing my mind.

How can you long for plain apple pie when you've landed in the middle of à la mode?

—Jenny

GLORIA'S HOUSE is all glass and angles and decks set in the middle of citrus trees and exotic tropicals I'd give my eyeteeth to have. Not that I can't grow mandevilla and bougainvillea in Mississippi, but I have to put them in pots and bring them inside during the winter. And I don't have space. Nor a greenhouse, which Rick's been promising to build but I'm not likely to get till hell freezes over, as they say.

As Gloria wheels her Ferrari into the curving driveway, the front door flies open and out pops a woman I can't even begin to describe. She's got this big red ponytail that looks like it's fake but just might be real, and she's wearing honest-to-goodness cat's-eye glasses that she may or may not need, studded with rhinestones that could be diamonds. What do I know? This is Hollywood.

I have to pinch myself.

"Hello, Roberta." Gloria waves and grins.

"Get your skinny butt out of the car and let me look at you."

"Not so skinny anymore, thanks to Jenny's Southern-fried chicken."

"Girl, I'm going to give you a medal." Roberta wraps me in a hug that nearly crushes bones, then stands back and looks me up and down like she's holding a microscope and I'm the bug. A good bug, I'd say from her grin.

"I've been trying to get her to put some meat on her bones for fifteen years." She whirls toward Angie. "And look what we got here. A real beauty. You're going to set this town on its ear."

"Thanks, but that's not likely with Mother looking over my shoulder every minute."

"Let me see if you've got any teeth?" Roberta tilts my daughter's head back and practically sticks her face down Angie's throat. "Uh-huh. If I'd talked to my mama like that I'd have been picking my teeth up off the sidewalk."

"Roberta." Gloria tosses her a tote bag. "Mind your manners."

"I don't have any to mind. Not a speck." Roberta chuckles as she marches into the house.

Gloria leads me into her house and I feel like one of those game-show contestants who has just won a fabulous week in Hollywood. Only this is a million times better. This is real. This is friendship.

"You'll get used to her," Gloria says.

"Get used to her? I love her."

My bedroom overlooks the swimming pool, but then every bedroom in this house does. Gloria's house must have been designed by an architect who loved the outdoors, because there's a view from every room, trees and flowers and wide-open blue sky that make you think everything's right with this world. Except you know it's not. You know children are going hungry and man is lifting up arms against man and somewhere in Mooreville, Mississippi, your husband is wondering why he ever married you.

After supper, Gloria and I sit beside the pool and watch Angie swim.

"This is so lovely. Thank you, Gloria."

"You're more than welcome."

"I want to help you while I'm here. Just tell me what I can do."

"You can sit by the pool with a good book and a tall glass of lemonade and listen to the birds. You can forget about helping everybody else and do something for yourself, for a change. Just relax, Jenny."

"I'm not sure I know how. Anyway, I feel I ought to be—oh, I don't know. Making sure Angie's not calling Jackson twenty million times a day and calling Rick to see if he's okay. I even worry about Godzilla. Not the old battle-ax, herself. I worry she's going to turn Rick against me. Permanently."

"Jenny, did you ever read those wonderful Winnie the Pooh books to Angie?"

"Yes. She had a whole menagerie of animals from the Hundred Acre Wood."

"What I love about Pooh is his ability to simply be in the moment."

"Is that what you're going to do, Gloria? Just be?"

"Heck, no. I can't afford to sit back and relax. I'm going to fight like a wildcat to get my TV role back. But then, my producer doesn't love me the way Rick loves you."

"You think?"

"I know."

Something about being on the west coast makes me believe her. Maybe it's the scent of orange blossoms.

CHAPTER 11

Nothing falls harder than ego.

—Gloria

The only reason I feel safe leaving Jenny and Angie alone is that this morning Roberta showed up acting like they were her long-lost best friends and if anybody so much as looked at them cross-eyed, she'd snatch some heads bald. Or worse.

Plus, she practically pushed me out the door.

"Go on." She handed me my hat, my briefcase, my sunglasses and my car keys. "Go see what your agent's got for you. I can handle things around here with one hand tied behind my back."

"I thought I'd take a day or two to rest, decompress."

"Well, you thought wrong. I made the appointment the day you finally informed me of your plans. Now get out of here. Me and Jenny have stuff to do."

"Jenny and I. Like what?"

"Like none of your business. Go on and let me take care of the entertainment aspect, Miss Perfect Grammar."

Now I'm fighting freeway traffic and wondering why I ever thought getting back into the Hollywood flow of things was the perfect idea. Sighing, I glance out the window. Cars are lined bumper to bumper in both directions as far as I can see, and drivers are acting as if their lives depend on setting the world's speed record in the next six blocks.

Mississippi never looked so good.

MORT LEVINGER greets me as if I'm his favorite client, which is part of Mort's effectiveness as an agent. He makes everybody feel as if they are his personal favorite.

"You're looking wonderful, Gloria. Sit down." He motions me toward an overstuffed brown leather chair, and as I sink into the soft cushions I have a crazy urge to curl up and go to sleep. Where's my focus? My never-give-up spirit?

"How are you feeling? No ill effects from your accident?"

"I'm perfectly fine. Good as new. Ready to work."

"That's my girl." Mort flips through a stack of papers on his desk and extracts a fat script. "Take a look at this. One of Bert Bogan's projects. He wants you for the role of Norma."

The movie is a drama titled *After the Rain*. I skim down the list of characters and find Norma near the bottom. An aging, bitter next-door neighbor to Wayne and Linda.

I can't believe this.

"A bit part?"

"I wouldn't call it that, Gloria."

"What would you call it?"

"An acting job. They're not that easy to find."

"You mean for a woman my age."

"I'm just being realistic. The key is to keep you working, Gloria. And this is a feature film, not TV. It's not unusual for an actress of your status to have to drop back a bit when she shifts to the larger screen."

I scan the script, looking for Norma's lines.

"Oh, here's a great line. 'Hello.' And how about

this one? 'I don't gossip.'" Flipping the pages, halfway between rage and panic, I discover that not only is Norma a bit part, but she has only two lines.

"Four words, Mort? Four words!"

"Look at it as keeping your foot in the door."

"What's the budget?"

"Low budget."

"How low?"

"Two million."

By Hollywood standards this is lower than a toad. I see my career vanishing while I sit in my chair, trying not to hyperventilate.

"You'll get a different kind of exposure with feature film, Gloria."

"What have I been for the last twenty years? Chopped liver?"

"Look, Gloria. Just give it some thought. That's all I ask. Meanwhile, I'll speak to Claude again about you returning to *Love in the Fast Lane*."

"You've already spoken with him?"

"He's looking to broaden the show's appeal to the younger set."

I promise to think about the deal, then tuck the script in my purse.

On the drive home I fight against defeat and humiliation, but emotions don't need permission, don't respond to logic.

They just *are*.

NOBODY'S HOME when I get there, which gives me a little time to regroup. I change into my swimsuit, then mix a pitcher of margaritas and take it along with the script poolside with the full intention of reading all the way through. Perhaps there's some redeeming feature in this role. Maybe Norma has some pivotal scene where she doesn't speak lines. Maybe she's hiding in a closet, witnesses a murder and is rendered speechless the rest of the movie.

One can only hope.

Speaking of hope, I race back inside to check my messages. Two from telemarketers and none from Mississippi. None that pop up on my caller ID as Matt Tucker, heartthrob.

"AS I LIVE and breathe. What have we got here?"

Roberta's loud bray nearly knocks me off my hammock. She grabs my towel off a deck chair and tosses it over me.

"Cover yourself up before you turn to a

lobster." Picking up the pitcher, she glares at the drink level. "Looks like we've had ourselves a little drunken brawl."

"I am not drunk. I've had only…" I can't remember how many drinks I've had. Enough to make me feel like the hammock is spinning. Enough to make me forget Norma, who hasn't witnessed anything except her expanding waistline and her graying hair. Almost enough to forget Tuck. "You can't have a brawl with only one person, Roberta."

"My point, exactly." She marches inside, comes back with a glass and pours herself a drink. "Now, how about you confess to Sister Roberta."

"The next thing I know, you'll be elevating yourself to sainthood. Where are Angie and Jenny?"

"Still shopping at Macy's. Having a ball. I'm going back to pick them up later, but I thought I'd better check on you. Looks like I was right."

"What tipped you off?"

"The only other times I've seen you looking like a hound dog who can't smell a rabbit is when those two scoundrels you called *husband* left you. Our drink of choice then was tequila." She lifts her glass. "I prefer margaritas. Congratulations on your improved taste."

"I've just lost my *career*, Roberta. And Mort wants me to play a frumpy, surly woman who never heard of bleached blond. A *bit* part."

"Oh yeah? You've had your ups and downs before. Remember that new director at *Love in the Fast Lane* who wanted you to get amnesia and turn into a bag lady?"

"By the time I finished with him, he was sending roses and chocolates to my dressing room, and on his knees apologizing."

"See, that's just what I mean. The only time you drink more than half a glass of anything is when you've got man troubles. So who is he?"

"There's no use trying to fool you."

"None whatsoever. Trouble brings out my dark side. Tell me who it is, and I'll snuff him out for you."

By the time I finish telling Roberta about Tuck—leaving out all the best parts, of course—she's drooling into her margarita.

"So how come you're sitting in that hammock instead of trying to capture Mr. Perfect? Wait. Don't answer. Let me take a wild guess. You've lost your tiny mind."

"Listen, Roberta. I'm not going to tuck my tail between my legs and run into the arms of the first man who looks twice at me just because I can't get a decent acting job. I came back here to reclaim my career."

"I saw a TV special where they talked about elective surgery. They lift your face right off. Just set it on the table somewhere then try to stitch it back in the right place. You could end up looking like Frankenstein."

"Who said anything about facelifts?"

"One woman had so many botched jobs, her skin looked like one of them dogs with the saggy skin. What're they called?"

"Shar-Pei. And it's *those* dogs, Roberta."

"Who gives a shit? All I'm saying is the femme fatals out here are younger than my tennis shoes."

"Okay, you've made your point." I take a sip of my drink. "And it's *femmes fatale*. Not *fatals*."

"One woman couldn't even shut her eyes to sleep."

"Roberta, I'm not having a facelift. And that's final."

"Well, good."

"Fine. Don't say another word."

"Pass the margaritas?"

She's grinning and I start laughing and can't stop. Sometimes this is all we have, the ability to laugh at ourselves, no matter what.

Mix a charge card with a vacation and you've got a miracle.

—Angie

IF I'D KNOWN Mom could be transformed by shopping in a different city, I'd have gone with her to all those malls she wanted to drag me to when we were vacationing in Myrtle Beach or Gulf Shores and I just wanted to lie on the sand and work on my tan.

She's in the dressing room trying on outfits, every one of them blue because Roberta told her they brought out the color of her eyes. She acted like it was news to her. You'd think she didn't even own a mirror.

Okay. So I'm not being quite fair here. Mom spends most of her time in the kitchen and the rest on the telephone drumming up support for her committees. I blame the committee thing squarely on her, but I'll have to say that if it weren't for the restaurant, she might do something besides bake forty different kinds of pies.

Dad ought to see that. I can tell you one thing: seeing Mom in Hollywood has opened my eyes, too. I'm not going to let Jackson—or any other man for that matter—stick me in a rut and leave me there. Women in ruts mold over.

Here comes Mom in a pretty linen two-piece dress with a swingy skirt.

"What do you think?"

Life as I know it has come to an end. She's asking my opinion. I almost look behind me to see who she's talking to, but Roberta's gone and so I know it's me.

"You've got great legs, Mom."

"I do?"

"Yeah. You ought to show them off more often."

"That settles it. I'm buying this dress."

I think I've been promoted to wardrobe mistress. A big step up from troublesome teen.

Wait till I tell Sally.

Or maybe I won't. Some people live their whole lives at the center of their own sad little dramas. I don't want to be like that. It would be nice for a change to be the one having a good time with a really cool mom.

If a one-man woman struts her stuff, will the seismic shift be heard all the way to Mississippi?

—Jenny

I CAN'T remember the last time I bought a dress with anything in mind except whether the neckline was high enough to pass muster at Bougefala Baptist Church. And I certainly can't remember the last time anybody commented on my legs.

My own daughter. I can hardly believe it.

I spread the dress on the bed in this guest room that looks like something out of *Architectural Digest*—skylights and interesting angles, furniture solid and expensive-looking without being fussy, soft sand colors accented with the amazing golds and pinks and purples of a sunset. Then I step into the shower. Roberta's taking Angie and me out to dinner. Somewhere fancy, was all she'd say.

Gloria was in bed with a headache when we got back from Macy's. How can you blame her? If I had a houseful of people up to their ears in problems, I'd go to bed, too.

She's a saint for taking us in. That's all I can say.

I step into the shower and enjoy the sheer luxury of standing under the water without having to worry about hurrying so I can cook supper. Gloria has these great big plush terry-cloth robes hanging on the door. *Just for guests*, she said. When I finish my bath I wrap myself up like a pampered princess and stroll barefoot to the French doors to watch the moon shining on her swimming pool.

It's beautiful here. What woman in her right mind wouldn't be happy?

Me. Silly me, who can't stop thinking about Rick.

When my cell phone beeps to let me know there's a call I missed, I run like I'm planning to jump into a lifeboat. And maybe I am. The caller ID shows Rick's name.

I press Listen.

"Jenny, where do you keep the clean sheets? The bed needs changing and I can't find them."

So much for lifeboats. In a knee-jerk reaction I start dialing, then stop. Just stop.

We've been married twenty-three years and

this man can't even find the sheets? Where does he think they come from? The little sheet fairies?

"Up yours, Rick. Find your own darned sheets."

Nobody hears me, but I feel better just saying it aloud. I look in the mirror, fluff up my hair, wonder how I'd look if I put in some red highlights, then march to the bed and put on the dress that makes my legs look six feet long.

Well, maybe not, but who's measuring? As long as people notice.

Heck, if a man notices tonight, I'm liable to notice him right back.

CHAPTER 12

If you don't plan to fool around, how far should a hand on the knee go? And where's the goddess code when you need it?

—Jenny

Oh...my...gosh. We're at the Magic Castle. This is a place I've only dreamed about, a private club where you can't even get in the parking lot, much less the door, unless you're a member or the guest of one. And to be a member you have to be a magician.

It turns out Roberta's husband Hubert, who is a retired electrical engineer, knows how to levitate his wife. And I'm not talking about sex, though from the way he's eyeing her, he probably does that, too. He's a hobby magician.

And so is his brother, Max, who just happens to be in town for the evening. Or so Roberta says.

Good lord, I think she's trying to set me up. The bad part is, I like it. Or maybe that's the good part, and the bad part is, I feel guilty. Like I'm going to jump between the sheets with this short bald man wearing a dark summer suit and a handlebar mustache. Really. I know he sounds awful but somehow he ends up being cute. Not like my drop-your-pants gorgeous Rick. More like some olive-skinned stranger who's not really all that good-looking but is a bit exotic and somehow sexy.

He kisses my hand when we meet, then leans close to hear what I have to say while we eat very tender steak in a beautiful dining room with soft lighting.

And what am I telling him?

"My husband Rick is a whiz with food. Owns his own restaurant. Built it from scratch. People come from all over northeast Mississippi just to see him. He was a local basketball star, and sports fans still see him as a celebrity."

I can't seem to shut up. Angie's looking pleased as pie that I'm talking about her daddy instead of plotting to betray him, and Roberta's watching me like I'm somebody who rolled off the watermelon truck and ought to know better.

"So, tell me about yourself, Max." I say this in my best imitation of Jillian Rockwell's goddess purr.

"Nothing I could say about me is nearly as interesting as you," he says.

I know it's a line and so does my daughter, who rolls her eyes. If we were home and heard some man say that on a TV movie, I'd giggle and she'd say *oh, puhleeze*.

Instead she begs off dessert and asks if she can be excused. I'm proud of her. For all her aggravating qualities, at least she has manners.

"Is it okay if I wait in the piano bar?"

I tell her it is. She's been intrigued by that bar ever since Roberta explained that Irma, the ghost pianist, takes requests. I'm sure it's just a player piano, but Roberta says you can call out a song and Irma will play it.

That's Hollywood for you. Full of tricks and surprises.

"Okay. We'll meet you there."

Actually I'm glad she's gone. How can I try out my new dress and test my goddess wiles while my teenage daughter watches?

After she leaves, Roberta says, "Jenny, tell Max about your roses."

Okay. I can talk about flowers. That seems safe enough. Not domestic. Maybe even a bit romantic.

"I don't have the wonderful California climate for roses, but with a lot of care and feeding plus heavy watering in our hot, dry summers, I grow some really nice varieties."

"What's your favorite color?" Max asks, and when I tell him pink, he reaches up and plucks a pink rose from the air.

"Ohmygosh. That's wonderful."

"You like that?" Max hands me the rose, then reaches behind my ear and plucks out a silver dollar.

Roberta's beaming and nodding, and I'm thinking that the Magic Castle is full of dark nooks and crannies where a hurting, unsure-of-herself woman from Mississippi might let a nice, sexy magician who pulls roses from the air hold her hand. Or more.

That's probably deprivation talking, but, lord, wouldn't a little male attention be nice? Even if I don't plan to do anything drastic. Wouldn't it be nice if I could feel attractive and interesting and worth a bit of effort? Just for one night?

It turns out Max is too much of a gentleman to put his hand on my knee, but when we leave the table he does put it on my elbow and guide me toward the piano bar.

I'm feeling pampered, and a bit mellow from the wine, and I admit to letting my hip brush against his.

Before Angie was born, Rick and I used to go outside on beautiful summer nights and have a glass of wine in the gazebo. I'd lean against him and we'd watch the stars. He knows the names of the constellations and which planets move closer to the moon at specific times of the year.

Rick has a magic all his own. Or at least he once had. I wonder if it's still there, hidden under layers of responsibility and neglect.

Not that I'm making excuses for him. I got caught up in diapers and he got caught up in building a business. Then we both immersed ourselves in Angie's activities—the elementary school plays where she was a sunflower or a tree or a rabbit, the painful piano recitals till she finally announced she hated music, the swim practices, swim meets and fundraisers for the swim team, all the hoopla of being a supportive parent.

And I don't regret a minute of it. Not one second. Still, I mourn for what we lost.

And I don't know how to get it back. Or even if I can.

"Mom." Angie spots me and trots over, dragging a scrawny-looking boy. "You've got to see this."

In a roped-off area, the piano keys are flying up and down as if invisible fingers are playing "Beale Street Blues."

"That's amazing. Did you request the song, Angie?"

"I'm not talking about the song. I'm talking about Marshall." Oh lord, what kind of boy is named Marshall?

"Watch this," she adds, and the gangly boy at her side proceeds to pull three balls out of nowhere and start juggling. Suddenly there are four balls, then five, then six.

Now I'm thinking she's going to run away to Las Vegas with Marshall where she'll spend the rest of her life in a box while he saws her in half.

And maybe that's what happens to all of us when we stop paying attention.

I'm just a foolish, overprotective mother. I brought her out here to have a great time, so why am I worried when she does?

"Marshall's doing a show in fifteen minutes," Angie tells us, "and he's going to call me onstage."

"That's great." I try to work up some enthusiasm, but she's too excited to pay me any attention.

When we leave the ghost of Irma behind and troop behind Marshall and Angie, I'm grateful for this: she hasn't pulled out her cell phone to call Jackson one single time since we got here. Okay, maybe they have signs that you can't use them in here. I didn't notice.

But I don't think she did. What I believe is that my daughter is finally getting a glimpse of possibilities outside Mooreville, Mississippi, and Jackson Tucker. And for that, I'm eternally grateful.

The showroom is one of the bigger ones, Max tells me as he deftly steers me toward a dark corner. I check to see that Roberta and Hubert are close behind. Not that I don't trust Max. But there's something heady about being in this place of magic. I'm not sure I trust myself.

As Marshall takes the stage, Max reaches for my hand. Here's the amazing thing. I don't like it. Not because of any guilty I'm-betraying-my-husband feelings, but because it doesn't feel right. The shape, the texture of his skin, the way his thumb feels as he makes circles in my palm. There's nothing sexy and exciting about it. It just tickles. And it doesn't make me feel interesting or cute or even halfway desirable.

It makes me believe he saw an opportunity and seized it. Not even because he wanted to, but because his sister-in-law expects it. Maybe Roberta even demanded it.

The thing I'm learning here is that holding hands is just two pieces of flesh bumping against each other unless there's a real connection between the people involved.

And the only connection I want is thousands of miles away.

Angie's on stage while Marshall pulls colored scarves out of her hair. Her smile makes everything worthwhile—the trip I didn't really want to make, the nights I've stayed awake watching the clock for her to come home, even the arguments with Rick over our many differences about what spoils a child.

This is just life, full of highs and lows with rare moments of gliding along on an even keel.

When she takes a bow, I pull my hand away from Max to applaud, and I don't let him have it again. Even when we end up back in the piano bar where he tries to recapture the mood by asking my favorite song. I lie and tell him I don't have one and he requests "Eternally," which is meant for people falling in love.

I'm already in love. With my husband. And that's forever.

The more I see, the less I discover I know.

—Angie

I THOUGHT I had it all figured out, but I never expected to meet Marshall tonight. Listen, contrary to what some people think, I'm no starry-eyed kid. I'm not talking about love at first sight or anything like that. All I'm saying is that he's a nice guy who's lots of fun. And he knows Tom Cruise. Honestly. His uncle worked on one of Tom's movie sets, and Marshall got to meet him.

And Marshall's got this neat group of friends he told me about and I'm dying to have over—one whose daddy is an astronaut, one who builds robots in her basement, and one who works summers with the marine life at Sea World in San Diego.

I never dreamed the world could be so big. The future I planned with Sally over double cheeseburgers with fries and talked about with Jackson in the back seat of my car has lost some of its appeal.

Sometimes I guess you have to leave home to find out what you really want.

When the world's unraveling and so are you, wear red lipstick. Fool everybody.

—Gloria

"I CAN'T believe you did that."

Roberta's sitting opposite me at the glass table in the sunroom, not the least bit contrite about her clandestine trip to the Magic Castle last night with my guests.

Furthermore, she's having a logger's breakfast of bacon and eggs and biscuits with sawmill gravy while I sip tomato juice, which is all my poor head will allow.

"You told me to be nice," she says. "I was being nice."

"You got me drunk so you could fix Jenny up with Max. Of all people."

"I didn't see you trying to resist that pitcher full of margaritas. And what's wrong with Max?"

"For one thing, you tried to set him up with me."

"And you're jealous?"

"Of course I'm not jealous. He's all hands. How could you do that to Jenny?"

"I didn't notice her complaining. And besides, I thought it would be good for her. And maybe make that husband of hers sit up and take notice."

"What did you do? Take pictures?"

"I didn't need to."

"Good lord. You're counting on Angie telling her father."

"I didn't roll in here off a watermelon rind."

"Watermelon *truck*."

"Who cares? At least I'm trying to fix things instead of setting on my skinny butt with a hangover."

"Sitting."

"You're going to be laid out flat if you don't shut up and get dressed. You've got an appointment with that old fox at the studio in about three hours."

"Good grief. Why didn't you tell me?"

"I guess because I'm crazy. I guess because I

wanted you to spoil my breakfast with a lecture and a grammar lesson. Oh, and by the way. You got a phone call from Mississippi while you were moaning and groaning in the shower this morning."

"You're fired."

"You've already fired me about two hundred and eighty times."

"Watch your step, or one of these days I'll mean it."

I race as fast as I can, which means I halfway hurry while holding onto my throbbing head. Roberta scrawled the message on my incoming calls log.

"Matt Tucker, Mooreville, MS. Sounds like Humphrey Bogart in his heyday with Lauren Bacall. You ought to take a lesson from Bacall's book. Let some of that hair fall down into one eye then seduce the pants off him."

Lord, Roberta's sassy ways and sassy notes have kept me smiling even when I felt as if the rest of the world was falling down around my ears. I owe her a bonus. And some roses. Someday Roberta's going to retire, and then who will I have?

I pat my hair into place, slash on red lipstick,

and try to get myself into a good mood. Then I pick up the phone and dial Tuck's number.

"Gloria?"

Lord, that mesmerizing, horse whisperer's voice. I have to sit down.

"How are you, Tuck?"

"I'm coming to Del Mar. Racing Tuck's Golden Boy."

I try to read between the lines, but can't. I don't know if it's because of the state of my head or the state of my heart.

"I'd like to see you, Gloria. Can you join me in my box?"

"When?"

"This Saturday. Noon."

"Yes."

Only one word. And I hope it's the right one. Saturday, we'll see.

First, though, I have to work a miracle so I can walk into the studio looking like America's favorite TV goddess.

Roberta wasn't kidding when she called the producer of *Love in the Fast Lane* an old fox. Three hours and the miracle of Max Factor later, I'm sitting opposite Claude Foxwort in his office, sometimes known as the fox's den, where people come to get their heads chewed off, and secretly known as the fox's lair where more than one nubile nymph has sought career advancement on the leopard-skin couch.

I loved everything about my job except Claude Foxwort. Sitting here now in a Vera Wang dress that shows I haven't lost my figure, with a tote bag full of fan mail that proves I haven't lost my viewer appeal, I try to keep my skin from crawling.

I've never had that kind of reaction to Claude. Before he wrecked my career and I wrecked my Ferrari, I handled him with amused tolerance. Suddenly I'm seeing him in stark contrast to Matt Tucker and Rick Miller. Even to Jackson Tucker. They were real men living real lives.

With his cleverly fitted toupee, his tanning-bed glow and his implanted pecs, Claude's as artificial as a Ken doll. All facade and no substance.

"You're looking rested, Gloria."

As compared to what? My haggard looks when I left the show?

"Thank you, Claude. So are you."

"So, Roberta said you wanted to see me."

"Yes. I wanted to show you a small sample of my fan mail." I place the bag on his desk. "This is about a tenth of the letters I've received, all demanding my return to the show."

He waves his hand, dismissing my best plan to regain my role as Jillian Rockwell.

"We've had some letters, too. I'll admit you were popular, Gloria, but the show was getting tired and old feeling. It needed a new look, new blood, fresh faces."

"You mean *young* faces."

"If you want to put it that way. Susan Star's really igniting the show. Bringing in a younger audience." He picks up a pencil and twirls it under his nose like a handlebar mustache, a little conceit I used to find funny and now find insufferable.

My lord, if I came back to here I don't know how I'd keep from slapping him silly. What was I thinking, anyhow? I've always lived by the philosophy that when one door closes an even better one opens. Never one to batter at closed doors, I've always moved on, alert to new opportunities.

I stand up and smooth my skirt. "I wish you luck with the show, Claude."

"Not so fast." He's now twirling the pencil like a majorette's baton. "We might bring you back in a different role, say Susan's favorite great aunt, somebody she occasionally confides in. With the right makeup and lighting, a little padding worn under your dresses, you could pass for sixty-five."

I want to jump over the desk and beat him with his Italian leather loafers. Instead, I take a deep breath and say, "No thank you, Claude," then gather my letters and march out.

My grandmother would be proud of me. It could be the best exit of my career.

Outside I sit in the hot sun resting my head against the steering wheel, gathering courage, marshalling my spirit. Roberta will be waiting back home to hear the news. So will Jenny and Angie.

I could turn this all into a big joke and leave them laughing. After all, I am an actress.

I back out of the parking lot and head toward North Hollywood, toward my friends who love me, no matter what.

Forget acting. I'm going to tell the unvarnished truth.

CHAPTER 13

Why is it easier to toot somebody else's horn?

—Jenny

I am incensed listening to Gloria's recital of Claude Foxwort's cheap offer to turn her into somebody else, somebody who would confuse and disappoint her fans and undermine everything she's built for us over the years.

"Why, you're our hero." I blurt this out, while Gloria sits, tense and quiet in the yellow chintz chair with the sun making gold streaks across her cheekbones. They look like knife blades. I almost envy her. If I looked like her instead of me, Rick wouldn't let me out of his sight.

I should be ashamed of myself. Really. Sitting here thinking about my own problems instead of hers.

"I ought to march down there and jerk a knot in that old fox's tail," I say, meaning it.

Angie, who usually thinks only of her own impossible teenage dreams, gets up in arms.

"Mom ought to organize a great big protest. She's good at that."

A week ago I'd think Angie meant that as an insult, but change seems to be working its magic. I really think she means it as a compliment, though I'll never know.

She's moved on to topics more interesting than the trials and tribulations of grown-ups.

While she prattles on to Gloria about Marshall, I mull over the possibilities of a protest. Forget that I don't know anybody in Los Angeles except Roberta and Gloria. Forget that I don't know my way to the corner store, let alone the studio where my favorite soap opera of twenty years is filmed.

I'm good at organizing, so good I've organized myself out of a marriage. Still, it's not only something to think about; it's something to fill my time, the long, lonely stretch of hours while I wait for heaven knows what.

A miracle?

Maybe I'll give this protest a whirl. If I can't

work a miracle for myself, please God, let me work one for the woman who is now telling my teenage daughter she doesn't recommend accepting Marshall-the-magician's offer for burgers and fries in parts unknown.

"Why don't you invite him over for a swim?" is the next part of Gloria's advice, which sounds reasonable to me. And safe.

"That way, we can get to know him," I say, and Angie makes a face as if I've just stepped in something foul.

"Come *on*, Mom. I'm not a baby. I don't need a chaperone."

It seems like I take one step forward with her and three steps back.

In Mooreville, I knew everybody. If Angie mentioned a boy, I not only knew his parents and where he lived, but I knew whether he went to church and how often. I knew if he had ambition or was just coasting along, looking for trouble.

"I just want to know if he's a nice boy." I turn to Roberta. "Hubert probably knows him. Can you ask your husband?"

"Next thing I know," Angie says, "you'll be calling the FBI."

"I already did, baby girl."

Roberta says this in a way that makes my daughter grin. Why can't I do that? Why do I always say the exact thing that will start a fight?

"You've got three chaperones," she adds. "Not one. But as pretty as you are, Marshall wouldn't notice us if we were a herd of elephants lined up at the patio door begging for peanuts."

"You're the best." Angie hugs Roberta and Gloria, then hesitates as if she thinks I might be carrying the black plague.

"I don't bite," I tell her, and she's grinning when she leans down to give me a peck on the cheek.

I wish I could tell Rick. *We're making progress here*, I'd say. *We're both learning the light touch*.

I wonder what would happen if we applied that touch to our marriage. If I laughed with Rick more and accused him less. If he accepted me as I am and expected less. Maybe there's no such thing as miracles that fall out of the sky. Maybe there are only miracles we make ourselves.

I stand up, the rest of the long day stretching before me.

"Well, who's in the mood for an apple pie?"

The fruit basket is filled with nice, tart Granny Smiths, and I know the cupboard is as well-stocked as Rick's restaurant. I've checked.

"If you go near that kitchen, I'll break both your arms," Roberta says.

"Okay, okay."

I don't go near the kitchen; I go to Universal Studios on the typical tourists' tour with Gloria while Angie stays home to swim and call her friends, including Jackson, I'm sure. But that doesn't even bother me now. Roberta stays behind to "shovel through a ton of you know what" in her office. Her words. Not mine.

Strolling around Universal's lot finding out that King Kong is made up of tricks and Gilligan's Island is little more than a small pond on a small lot, I feel a sense of loss. What I love about the movies is the sense I'm watching something magical.

Listen, I know this is silly, but when I was ten I still believed in fairies. And unicorns. And Cinderella finding her Prince Charming.

In a way, I still believe in those things. I just don't know how to recapture the feeling of magic in a world of pie crusts and dog poop and Wet Jet mops.

"I don't want to make pies anymore."

"What?"

Gloria and I have moved on past the sharks that won't bite, the Red Sea that's not a sea, and the Psycho house. We're standing in a gift shop in front of the *Wizard of Oz* display.

"I love cooking. I love that Rick's customers enjoy my pies. But I'm tired of being separated from him all day."

"Have you told him?"

"No."

I guess couples get so used to each other, we think our partner can read our minds. We forget how to say the important things. We hide the truth because it might cause change, and change is hard.

"There are a few things I haven't told Tuck, either. But I plan to."

She tells me about the invitation to Del Mar, and I click my heels together as if I'm wearing the Ruby slippers and have discovered the magic of home.

She ends up buying two small hand puppets from the Oz collection.

"One for you and one for me," she says.

Both are the Cowardly Lion. They're cute and cuddly with big medals pinned over their hearts that say Courage. Wearing our puppets on our hands, we link arms and head toward her Ferrari.

Leaning back against the leather seats I suddenly feel as if I can go anywhere. Even into a future that holds a little magic.

Is it possible Mom was once young?

—Angie

WHEN Mom walks in wearing this Cowardly Lion hand puppet and a grin that makes her look ten years younger, I can't believe it.

Something else I can't believe. She kicks off her shoes, rolls up her pants legs and dangles her feet in the swimming pool, even though there's water everywhere and she's getting the back of her slacks wet.

"Hey, you," she says and I say hey right back. "Did you get in touch with your friends?"

So that's her ploy. She wants to find out if I talked to Jackson.

"Yep. Marshall's coming over later. I talked to Sally, too. And Jackson."

Brace yourself. Here comes the tsunami.

"Is everything all right back home?"

Wonder of wonders. I think this California air is making Mom soft. Or maybe it's old age.

"Mom? When you were young, what did you dream about?"

"Your dad."

"Besides him."

She sighs. "I'm afraid I wasn't very ambitious."

"Come on, Mom. You must have wanted to do something?"

"A party planner. That's what I wanted to be." She leans down to splash me. "Sorry to disappoint you, kiddo."

I feel like a mean old Grinch who has stolen her Christmas.

"I think it's cool. And I'll bet you were good at it."

"Once upon a time." She gets up, feels the seat of her pants and says, "Whoops. Look at me."

As she goes inside, I resolve to be nicer to my mom. Even adults need affirmation.

If I leave the safety of the known, will I tumble or will I fly?

—Gloria

I LEFT this morning with my mind at ease. Of

course, Roberta's going to run the fort while I'm gone. She always does.

Still it's my guests I'm thinking about. But Jenny's finally relaxing, and Angie's scrapbooking and making new friends. Marshall's a nice kid.

Both the Millers stood in the driveway waving when I left. Angie even handed me a card she'd painted herself. A blue bird, flying over a little village that looked like Mooreville.

"Thank you for showing me how to fly," she's written, then "Love, Angie."

Love. I like to think she means that. And I like to think she has her feet more solidly on the ground, and that maybe I've played a small role in her growing up.

I hope so. If I have helped Jenny and her daughter, then it's more than I've accomplished in twenty years on TV. Scary thought.

I enter the city limits and the excitement of seeing historic Del Mar Race Track takes my mind off everything.

Built in 1937, this track was the brainchild of Bing Crosby, Pat O'Brien and Paramount Studios. The old-time greats, including Lucille

Ball, Desi Arnaz, Dorothy Lamour and Ava Gardner, graced its stands.

As I park my car and make my way among the crowd in the grandstand built in Spanish Mission style, I sense the mystique of the track's Hollywood past. And I feel a part of it all.

Up ahead I see Tuck in his owner's box, binoculars in his hands, scanning the crowd. Looking for me?

I duck behind a post, not ready to see him yet, not sure what I'll say or even what I want. Reaching into my tote for the program, I pull out the Cowardly Lion.

Just speak your heart. That's what I imagine he'd say if he could talk.

"Gloria." Suddenly Tuck's hand is on my arm, his solid six feet pressed close in the crowd. "Are you okay?"

"I think so." Courage. Truth. "Did you see me hiding?"

"Who can blame you? I'd hide, too, if I were you. Let's get something to drink." He steers me deftly back through the crowd, our bodies touching, a necessity with throngs of people milling about. Mine is on fire.

His? Who knows? I can't see his face without stopping mid-throng and causing a major collision.

In the dim light and coolness of the lounge, he says, "Margaritas all right with you?" then orders two and leads me to a corner booth. We sit elbow to elbow. Sip our drinks. Look at each other without embarrassment and with a great deal of curiosity.

And rampaging desire.

Now I see his clearly. In the darkening of his eyes, the intense way he has of seeing past my skin and bones all the way to my heart.

He reaches for my hand, turns it over, kisses each fingertip then lets his lips linger against the deep groove in my palm. It's called the heart line, and not without reason. His kiss sears through my skin, my bones, my racing blood and brands my heart.

"I'm selfish," he says.

"No. You're a courageous man who raised a son alone, built a racing empire and kept your feet on the ground."

"I wanted you all to myself. You're a strong, desirable, talented woman. I'll always want you all to myself."

I can't breathe, can't think, may never have another coherent thought in my life. Only this. Tuck. Just his name. Like a whisper. A song. A star.

"When you were in Mississippi, I made the same mistake with you that I made with Jolene. My ex-wife."

There's no thought of pretending. Courage and truth are my two new mottos.

"Jenny told me she was an opera star who returned to her career."

"I wanted her to choose me. I wanted all or nothing at all." He kisses my palm again, and thank God, *thank God*, he doesn't let go. "That's what I wanted of you. I was so jealous at the barbecue when the reporters came. I was arrogant and foolish enough to think you'd give up being the nation's TV goddess for a horse farm in Mooreville, Mississippi."

I could say something like, *You don't do yourself justice*. I could wax eloquent about Tuck's Farms and claim I'd like nothing better than to spend the rest of my life there.

Instead, I cut to the heart of the matter.

"Do you still feel that way?"

"About you? Yes. About choosing me? No.

You've worked as hard for your success as I have for mine."

I take back my hands, wrap them around the glass. Distant and guarded.

"Tuck, you're looking at the former goddess of daytime TV." I tell him about being replaced by a younger woman, my unsuccessful attempts to regain my spotlight. The funny thing is, in the telling I don't feel like a failure; I don't feel like a woman who has lost a career.

Instead, I feel as if I'm on the brink of something new, a woman stepping through one door and peering behind three more to see what she'll discover.

He recaptures my hand, holds on. His touch feels true and safe, and I try to explain the rest, the feeling of being poised for a different future but still uncertain what that future is.

"I'd like to tag along while you find out."

"I'd like that, too."

"Good. Now let's go to the stables so you can meet Tuck's Golden Boy."

I'VE NEVER seen a more beautiful horse, a more beautiful day. Surrounded by the smells of hay and horses, sweat and nerves, anxiety and hope, I fall completely into the moment.

Tuck lets me pet the stallion's soft muzzle, and introduces me to the jockey, Ramon, a tiny, dark-eyed man in the purple silks of Tuck's Farms. I also meet the stable boys and his assistant trainer, Largo Johnson, a big, gentle man I trust on sight.

There's a whole world here I've never imagined. I can see how it sucks you in, demands loyalty, commitment and total immersion.

Those are the qualities I see in Tuck as he pulls his jockey aside to talk about the horse, its needs, its quirks, its fighting spirit.

"You'll have to hold him back, Ramon. He wants to burst out of the gate running wide open. Talk to him, tell him he's winning, he's a champion. Talk him over the finish line. First."

After Ramon leaves, I say, "You really talk to horses like that? And they understand?"

"Who knows what goes on in the mind of another creature? Even humans."

He touches my hair, caresses my head, not the least bit self-conscious when he sees Ramon and the stable boys watching.

"The next time you're in Mississippi, I'll show

you. I have a lovely little filly named Moonchild who's eager to talk to a genuine star."

He leans close, whispers, "You're a star, Gloria. Always," then kisses me in full view of a growing and very interested crowd.

When a flashbulb pops, I expect him to whisk me off to some secret, dark stable no reporters would dare invade. Instead he turns to them and says, "This is Gloria Hart. My girl."

Then he whisks me away.

CHAPTER 14

If life gets good for your friends, does some of it rub off on you?

—Jenny

I couldn't be happier if it were happening to me. Really.

I'm sitting in Gloria's kitchen with a cup of coffee and the Sunday-morning paper spread on the table. Her picture is all over the news—in the society pages, in the sports pages. With Tuck. The two of them kissing at the Del Mar stables under headlines that scream, My Girl! Both of them with a gorgeous race horse covered with a blanket of roses under headlines proclaiming, Tuck and the Goddess: In the Winner's Circle. The million-dollar Pacific Classic winner's circle.

The two of them dressed to the nines, dancing under the headline, Is it Love? Horse Racing's

Most Eligible Bachelor and America's Sexiest TV Star.

When my cell phone rings, my heart does the cha-cha, then settles down when I see it's Roberta and not Rick.

"Holy sweet moly. If she don't run off with that hunka hunka burning love, I will myself."

"Isn't it great, Roberta? Looks like they patched things up."

"Why didn't you tell me they made men like that down there in the Deep South? I'm planning my retirement. Right next door to you."

"What about Hubert?"

"He can come, too, if he'll pull something out of his magician's robes besides that darned old rabbit."

"Roberta, you can't retire till we complete our plan."

"How's it coming? You up to your ears in phone calls?"

"Yes. And Marshall. Every time I turn around, he's here."

"Sounds like she's spreading her wings."

"Thank goodness. Angie's only called Jackson once in the last two days."

"She's a good kid, Jenny. Just hang loose."

"I'm trying. Listen, I know you're used to seeing this kind of publicity, but don't you think it gives our little scheme a boost?"

"Boost, my butt. It shoots us straight over the goal line. You got your tough skin on?"

I reach into the pocket of my robe, pull out the Cowardly Lion, start to say *I'm trying*, then change to a resounding, definitive *yes*.

When we say goodbye, I refresh my coffee, blow kisses toward the morning paper then pad barefoot down the hallway to check on Angie. She looks like an innocent kitten, curled into a little ball hugging her ancient, love-tattered teddy bear, Henry.

"Mom?" She opens one eye and peers at me. Mostly curious. "Anything wrong?"

"No. Just checking." Again. But I don't tell her that. She went out with Marshall and his friends last night for the first time instead of having Marshall come here. I didn't sleep a wink until she got home. Shortly past midnight.

I wait for the usual stinging zingers—she's old enough to take care of herself, I've probably hired the FBI, I don't trust her enough.

Instead she says, "I'm okay. Thanks, Mom." She's settling back into her nest of covers when the cell phone in my pocket rings. "Dad?" She sits up, rubbing her eyes.

I glance at the caller ID. "Yes."

Wide awake now, she bounds across the room and grabs the phone. "Hello. Dad?"

Sigh. At least I have a daughter who loves her father, and vice versa.

I'm a lucky woman. I know this.

Then why am I feeling sad and lonely and angry? I'll admit it. Seeing Gloria and Tuck I felt a flash of anger. Not at them, but at love in general, love that sprinkles some people with fairy dust and the rest of us with plain old dirt.

I stand in the doorway. Vacillating. Trying to decide whether to leave or stay, whether Rick will want to talk to me, too, whether Angie will think I'm eavesdropping, whether I'm a terrible mother, an even worse wife.

One thing I know; I'm a good friend.

Just as I'm turning to go, Angie hands me the phone. "Dad wants to talk to you."

I might as well have won the darned million-dollar Pacific Classic, myself.

"Hello? Rick?"

"I saw the coverage of the Del Mar races. I'm glad Gloria and Tuck worked things out."

"So am I." Angie's sitting up in bed, watching. I give her a cheery, two-fingered wave, then ease down the hall. Hopeful.

"Angie sounds like she's having fun."

"Yes. She loves it out here."

"Good." I could drive a Peterbilt rig through his silence. Finally he says, "What about you?"

In an attempt to stop myself from telling him how much I need him, I reach into my pocket and rub the belly of my lion.

"I'm good, Rick. How are you?"

"Fine." Two phantom Peterbilts fill this screaming silence. "The restaurant's doing well."

"Good. That's good."

"Well, Jenny. I guess you have things to do."

"Yes. Definitely."

"Hug Angie for me."

"Will do."

My hands are shaking when I drop the cell phone back in my pocket. At least he didn't ask the whereabouts of his socks. His razor. His sheets.

Oh lord, those empty sheets.

I push open the patio doors, race toward the citrus trees and spill my anguish on the orange blossoms.

I imagine people who experience what I have become so light they float off like colored balloons.
—Gloria

THE LONG French windows are open to fresh breezes, the smell of the ocean and the faint pink of the sunrise. Lying beside Tuck, his right arm holding me close, I see how it would be possible to chuck everything for this man.

"Gloria?" His voice is full of sleep. "Are you okay?"

"Better than okay." I turn, cup his face, savor the feel of morning stubble, the enchantment of the cleft in his square chin, the taste of deep dreams in his upward curving mouth.

Without a word he finds me under the covers; we find each other.

The rising dawn paints us with gold and we wear each other for a very long time.

Afterward, Tuck orders room service and we sit on the balcony in the sun, leaned back in wrought-iron chairs, our feet propped on an empty chair between us, toes and heels touching.

When he asks if I can stay one more day, I tell him yes. Without hesitation. Without reservation.

His foot caresses mine. "I don't want to disrupt your schedule."

What's a schedule compared to this paradise?

"Roberta can handle everything. Jenny and Angie love her. They'll be fine without me."

"Good." He peels an orange, feeds me sections, kisses the juice from my lips. "I want you to come to Mooreville. Soon."

"For how long?"

"As long as you can stay."

I settle back, savor the sun on my skin, the scent of the ocean, the taste of orange juice and kisses.

Today I will not think; I will simply *be*.

If I become somebody else, somebody with guts and a kick-butt attitude, will anybody know the difference? Will I?

—Jenny

I CAN PICTURE my obituary: Jenny Miller leaves behind her daughter who finally grew up, her husband who never knew he had a jewel, and her telephone.

After bawling all over the orange blossoms, I'm back in Gloria's kitchen trying to whip up enthusiasm among her fans for a huge "Bring Jillian Back" rally. I'd probably still be out in the backyard ruining the flowers if Gloria hadn't called my cell phone.

"Tuck wants me to stay one more day," is what she said, but it sounded like a question to me. It sounded like she was saying *I want to stay but I can't because I feel guilty not coming back to see about you.*.

"Fabulous!" I told her, and meant it. For one thing, it gives me more time to work out the kinks of the rally. In spite of this big fan list Roberta provided, I'm discovering that people in Hollywood seem to be busier than people in Mooreville.

Or maybe it's because they don't know me, they don't know I'd never ask them to cancel hair appointments and spa treatments unless it was for a good cause.

Friendship. The best cause I know.

And that's what I'm now on the phone telling Carol Shultz, who just happens to be secretary to the North Hollywood branch of Gloria's fan club.

"We need to do this because Gloria's character

Jillian has been our friend for twenty years. She's the incredible, smart, sassy woman we'd all like to be. She's our role model, and we need to fight for her."

It seems Carol has everything going wrong except hang nails and bad breath. I try to be sympathetic, but when Angie walks into the kitchen, she freezes into a pose of mock horror, clutching her heart. "What's wrong, Mom?"

"What tipped you off? Me banging down the receiver?"

"Your face. You look like you could bite tenpenny nails."

I hand Angie my list. "I've called half this list and only thirty people have committed."

"Well, Dorothy, this is not Kansas." Angie plops into a chair beside me, grinning.

I get a glimpse of how it might be with us—mother and daughter laughing together as I sail into old age and she floats into adulthood.

"Do you have any ideas?"

"Mom? Are you serious?"

"Well…yeah." I've surprised both of us.

"You bet I do." She whips out her cell phone.

"What are you doing?"

"Calling in the troops."

The troops turn out to be Marshall and friends. Two hours later we're all gathered around the pool, cell phones hot, as they rally Hollywood's teens to Gloria's cause.

I wish Rick could see this. Especially the part where Angie introduces me and sounds proud that I'm her mom. Especially the part where I'm seeing her as a person instead of an angst-driven teenage daughter bent on wrecking my sanity.

Roberta arrives mid afternoon and orders pizzas for everybody.

"Compliments of Miss Gloria Hart," she yells, and the kids stomp, whistle and yell their approval.

"Come on, Jenny. Let's get something cool. Looks like the war room can manage fine without two old farts." Roberta drags me into the kitchen and proceeds to mix a drink that knocks off the top of my head.

"My gosh, what did you put in this thing?"

"You don't want to know."

I guess not. And I guess I'm turning into a woman who knocks back drinks strong enough to fell a bull in the middle of a Sunday afternoon. The ladies at Bougefala Baptist Church would be scandalized.

"How'd you know what was going on?" I ask.

"A little bird told me."

"Angie?"

"That girl's got plenty of her mama in her."

"Oh, lord, I hope not. I hope she's just like Rick."

"Will you listen to an old coot who's got a Hollywood goddess twisted around her little finger and her husband still chasing her around the kitchen table?"

"Hubert chases you around the table?"

"When his arthritis is not acting up and his pecker's working."

I nearly choke. "I can't believe you said that."

"Take yourself lightly. That's my motto. Now, you want to hear me?"

"I'm all ears."

"It's time for you to quit acting like a doormat and strut out there and show your stuff."

"What stuff?"

"Any stuff you want. You can do anything you want to, Jenny. But it's up to you to figure out what you want."

"Rick."

Roberta gives me a look over her glass that says, *oh, yeah?*

Maybe she's right. If I climb out of the box I'm in, maybe I'll discover more than Rick Miller. Maybe I'll discover myself.

Who's the fox now?

—Gloria

DRIVING back home I feel as if I've been gone three months instead of three days. Amazing how wonderful it feels to let go and savor the moment.

My cell rings, reminding me the problems I left behind are still there, waiting. Funny, though, they no longer feel like big elephants sitting all over my living room. They're smaller now, reduced to a manageable size. Maybe a rat terrier gnawing on a shoestring.

"Where are you?" It's Roberta calling. Shouting, as usual. I wonder if she's hard of hearing.

"Twenty minutes from home. Is Jenny okay? Angie?"

"Forget about home. You've got to get down to the studio. Pronto."

"Oh no! Did you set up a meeting? Why didn't you tell me earlier? I'm not dressed for that."

"What are you wearing? Something sexy?"

I glance at my slim black Audrey Hepburn pants, gold sling-back heels, hot-pink spaghetti-strap top, gold bangles on my arms.

My good luck, go-get-'em emerald.

"You could say that." I narrow my eyes as if the incorrigible Roberta is in the car. "If you're thinking about that leopard-skin casting couch, you're out of your mind. I wouldn't touch that troglodyte with a ten-foot pole. And I certainly wouldn't resort to such sleazy tactics. What's gotten into you?"

She just laughs. Cackles, is more like it.

"Same thing that's got into you, probably. Did you have fun?"

"I ought to say 'None of your business.' But yes, I had fun. More than fun."

How do you explain amazement?

"Good. We're going to keep the good times rolling. Did you pack one of them long chiffon scarves?"

"Yes." Roberta has me so intrigued I don't even correct her grammar.

"Before you get out of the car, throw it around your neck."

"Why?"

"So you'll look like old Hollywood glamour."

"Because?"

"I'm through answering silly questions."

Roberta hangs up. I ought to fire her. For real. But where else would I find somebody who can mother me, make me laugh, manage my career and keep me grounded, all at the same time?

I pull into the parking lot behind the studio, rummage in my suitcase till I find a long diaphanous scarf that floats along behind me like a rainbow, then head around the side to the front entrance.

"Jill-i-an, Jill-i-an, Jill-i-an."

Following the sound of chanting I come upon the throng in front of the studio, carrying placards and wearing sandwich boards.

I am overwhelmed. Fumbling in my shoulder bag, I pull out big Jackie-O sunglasses. They're prescription and now I see the signs: Bring Back Jillian, We Want Jillian, Give Us Our Goddess.

I also see faces—Jenny, Angie and Roberta, front and center.

"Look, there she is," Angie yells, and this huge, wonderful crowd surges forward shouting, "We love you, Jillian. We love you."

I sign sandwich boards, placards, notepads, dry-cleaning slips. Even movie-ticket stubs.

Roberta sidles up. “Having fun?” I nod, and she proceeds to give orders. Through a megaphone, no less.

“Gloria will sign something for every one of you. First, let’s get back to our posts and get that stubborn old fox out here.”

When the mob surges back, I ask, “Did you do all this?”

Roberta nods toward Jenny and Angie. “Those two.”

“Angie helped?”

“Didn’t you notice all them teenagers?”

“That’s remarkable.”

“How come you didn’t correct my grammar?”

“You’ve known the difference all along?” Roberta nods, grinning.

“Then why do you insist on slaying the English language?”

“Just to get your goat. And to give you somebody to take care of.”

Roberta pats my hand, then hurries back toward Jenny. I am thunderstruck. At long last, Roberta has revealed that big heart I always suspected lay underneath her curmudgeonly exterior.

I need to give her a raise. And I should ask her about retirement.

Right now, though, all I have time for is a quick hug. Reporters are streaming this way shouting questions, and hard on their heels is none other than Claude Foxwort, himself.

"Miss Hart, are you coming back to the show?"

"Is it true your fans are planning all-night vigils at Claude Foxwort's home?"

"How do you account for your popularity with teens?"

Roberta punches me. "How does it feel to be back in the limelight?"

I don't have time to answer her, or even to think about that because Claude has barreled his way through the reporters and is standing by me like a guardian bulldog.

"We'll answer your questions one at a time." Obviously he's laboring under the impression that when he speaks, everybody listens.

Instead, Rita Gaines of *Reel News* elbows him aside and says, "Miss Hart, are you engaged to Matt Tucker?"

I start to say no, but Roberta punches me and says, "No comment."

"Is it true you'll be moving to Mississippi?"

Roberta digs her elbow into my side to shut me up. "No comment."

"*Are* you coming back to the show?"

Now Claude Foxwort's the one taking over. "*Of course*, she's coming back to the show."

If he thinks I'm playing Lolita's doddery old aunt, he has another think coming, as Roberta would say.

Rita Gaines, who is both revered and despised for her persistence, says, "As Jillian Rockwell?"

"Of *course*. We wouldn't dream of disappointing her legions of fans."

"Miss Hart, why did you leave the show? Did Tuck have anything to do with that?"

When Claude holds up his hand, the glare from his gaudy pinky-ring diamond nearly blinds me.

"That's enough for today. Miss Hart and I have an important meeting."

"We do?" When Roberta elbows me again, I figure I'm going to be black and blue. I also rethink her raise.

The reporters keep firing questions, and when we ignore them, they turn toward the eager fans to see what juicy tidbits they can gather.

"Go on," she says. "I'll take care of things out here."

"What about those autographs I promised?"

"We'll all wait for you in the commissary. Drinks and snacks on the studio."

Claude and Roberta square off like boxers in a national heavyweight championship. Finally, he says, "Done," and she says, "Good."

I'm getting ready to tell him thank you, but the Great One, who obviously reads minds, steps on my toe and shoos me away.

But not before she pokes me in the ribs and says, "Don't you get soft. You've got the upper hand, girl. Keep it. No matter what."

CHAPTER 15

If you're lost at sea, how do you know which direction is home?

—Gloria

In Claude's office I sink into a chair and rub my sore spots while the fox retreats behind his desk.

"That demonstration was impressive," he says, and I just nod.

Another trick I learned from Roberta. Don't tip your hand; don't give the enemy any ammunition. Listen and learn. Then act.

"So, how would you feel about coming back to the show?" I wait. "We've been taking another look at ratings and demographics. The fact is, Gloria, you have a cross-generational appeal."

Translated: when the show started catering to the diaper set, we lost our fan base.

"You're lost at sea, so it will be easy to find you,

maybe in a remote little Polynesian village. Something romantic with coconut trees and lots of beach. Of course, it will take a while. We'll want to do a big story buildup."

He's offering everything I wanted, everything I came back to Hollywood to fight for. Now I'm not so sure.

"I'll think about it, Claude."

Leaving his office, I head toward the cafeteria to find Roberta. She's going to ask me if I've lost my mind.

When she sees me, she trots over. "Well?" I tell her everything, and she just stands there laughing.

"What?" I ask.

"Perfect. You've just got yourself a great big raise."

It's not a raise I'm thinking about: it's a certain horse whisperer in Mooreville, Mississippi.

When you first emerge from your cocoon, people wearing blinders never notice you've become a butterfly.

—Jenny

ANGIE and Gloria and Roberta are in the kitchen drinking lemonade and congratulating each other on the success of today's rally. You'd think I'd be right in the middle, but I'm holed up in the bedroom.

I told them I needed to rest, but that's only partially true. Sure, spearheading such a huge event in a town where people don't even know me was more draining than I expected. But that's not why I'm so tired.

We'll soon be going home.

Angie has to get ready for her senior year. And me? I don't know what's waiting in Mooreville. Or whether Rick even wants me to come back.

Worse, will he leave if I do?

And why am I cowering in here waiting on him to tell me?

I dial his cell phone. Never mind the different time zones and the way the late-lunch crowd makes the middle of the afternoon a hectic time for him. Usually the early crowd cleans the buffet out of meat loaf and Rick's scrambling to replace it with fried chicken.

And I don't even know what he's doing about pies.

He answers, sounding out of sorts till he hears me, then he says "Hey," in that way of his that's friendly and sexy at the same time.

Will there ever be another Rick Miller? Will there even *be* Rick Miller?

"Angie and I will be coming home soon."

"I know. Sounds like the trip's been good for her."

"Has it been good for us, Rick?"

"What are you asking me, Jenny?"

"I guess I'm asking if you still love me."

His silence is so big I want to kill him.

"You needn't get so excited, Rick. It's not good for your heart." And it's certainly not good for mine, this appalling lack of interest on his part.

"Don't do this."

"Do what? Talk to you on the phone?"

"Start a fight."

"I'm not trying to start a fight. I'm just trying to find out if my husband wants me to come home."

While I wait long enough for Hannibal to cross the Alps with his army of bull elephants, I start making a mental list of things I'll keep during the divorce. My mother's china. My grandmother's rocking chair. The scrapbook with all Angie's little notes and drawings from the time she first discovered pencil and paper. She was three, I think.

He'll have to pry those from my cold, dead hand.

"Of course, you're coming home. I don't want Angie flying cross-country by herself."

"She's *seventeen*, Rick."

How things have changed. Usually it's Rick reminding me that Angie's growing up and I should trust her.

"I have to go, Jenny. They're calling me in the kitchen." He's not making this up. I hear the banging of pots, the rumble of frustrated staff in the background. "Let me know your travel arrangements."

That's another thing he'll have to pry from me with a crowbar. If he thinks he can act like I'm an afterthought then expect me to do my good-little-wife duties, as usual, he's hunting with the wrong dog.

Tossing the cell phone into a dresser drawer, I prance out to join the celebration.

It turns out the only celebrant in the kitchen is Gloria. Roberta has gone home, and Angie's gone out with Marshall.

"She said she'd be back by twelve," Gloria says, and I just nod, which goes to show I've learned how to leap tall buildings in a single bound.

But apparently I still haven't learned to be a goddess. Or anything close.

When I tell Gloria about the phone call, she asks if I told Rick how *I* feel.

Well, naturally not. I'm not used to telling other people how I feel. Most of the time, I don't even know myself. When you get used to being the one to carry on, you forget *emotional landscape* is even part of your map.

Besides, I know better than to expect sweet and cuddly when Rick's on the defensive. Good grief, even I have been known to say a word when somebody backs me against a wall. Once I told Godzilla to butt the heck out of my marriage, which is the closest I've ever come to a four-letter word.

"I don't know what I'm going to do, Gloria."

"Why don't you stay here? I'll fly home with Angie."

"Rick would probably head straight to a lawyer. He's expecting me to come home."

"He might surprise you, Jenny. What if he's as uncertain as you? What if he just needs a little encouragement?"

"When you get back, see if Tuck has a cattle prod. That ought to do the trick."

I swear, if you could bottle giggles with a girlfriend and sell them, you could cure all kinds of ailments. Loneliness. Uncertainty. Fear. Even heartbreak.

"It certainly worked with Claude," Gloria says.

"Have you decided what you're going to do?"

"I don't have the slightest idea. But I want to spend some time with Tuck before I decide."

See? This is the thing I'm talking about. If an icon like Gloria can be lured away from fame and fortune by love, a woman with nothing to brag about except lemon ice box pie doesn't stand a chance.

Tuck calls and when Gloria walks onto the patio for some privacy, I refill my glass then wander into the bathroom. See myself in the mirror. Really *see*.

Here's the thing: I'm not the prettiest woman on the block but I'm not half bad. I have shiny hair and a pleasant face, a nice smile. And I'm a kind person. Everybody says so.

Except Rick.

He used to, though. "Jenny," he'd tell me when

we were first married, "you're the sweetest woman I've ever known."

Of course, that's compared to Godzilla, but still, maybe he needs to remember how he once thought I was wonderful.

And maybe I need to stay in California to figure out what I'll do if he does remember. The truth is, I'm not the same woman he married, and if he wants me as I was, then I have an uphill battle convincing him to take me as I am.

If they ever do give classes in how to be an adult, I would like them to teach that saying goodbye is not a bad thing. Change is necessary for growth.

—Angie

I'M HAVING to pinch myself. All my new friends are at Gloria's house for a giant thank-you pool party. Actually, it's also my going-away party.

We're flying home to Mississippi tomorrow. Just Gloria and me.

Before I came to Hollywood, this would have flipped me out, but I've learned something out here: Mom's a person, too. With her own feelings, her own set of needs and *everything*. If she needs some time to work things out with Dad, it's not up to me to pout and whine and insist she fly home.

Besides, I don't want her to go back and bury herself in pie dough again. I like her better the way she is now. She's really *there*, you know what I mean? It's not like it used to be when she'd be in the house but you'd hardly ever know it unless she decided to lecture you about something or tell you to get off the telephone.

I'm not worried about what to tell Dad, either. What they say to each other is between them.

It's not like I'm a kid anymore. I can't have it both ways; I can't be practically a grownup enjoying a few freedoms and a little girl whining about divorce.

Listen, I help put together a rally that swayed a big-shot TV producer. I can handle anything. If anybody has any doubts, I'll just whip out my scrapbook.

Marshall's calling me to the deep end of the pool to show off my swan dive. In Mooreville, being on the swim team was just something I did. Out here, it's like I'm a contender for the U.S. Olympics.

I do a porpoise move that shoots me underwater where I propel my way to him with a speed that causes him to say, "You're amazing."

Sometimes I even amaze myself. Lately I can swim in the deep end whether I'm in the water or not.

CHAPTER 16

Does driving a Ferrari mean you've arrived? And how can you arrive if you don't know where you're going?

—Jenny

Gloria left me the keys to her Ferrari. As if I'm fixing to get in that dangerous machine and squirt around on freeways that make me pee in my pants—and that's just when I'm a passenger.

Still, it's not as bad as I thought, being here in her house all by myself. I pictured drawing the blinds after Gloria and Angie flew out of LAX this morning, crawling into bed and spending the rest of my life with the covers pulled over my head.

The thing about turning into a lion is that it's hard to be brave when you're by yourself. It's hard to talk yourself into believing you've made a right and justified decision when your friend is not there shaking the pom-poms, shouting encouragement and pouring tequila in your cup.

Besides, what am I going to do with all this time now that Angie and Gloria are gone? Even Roberta's not here. She and Hubert have gone to San Francisco to visit their daughter Beverly and her three little hellions. Roberta's words. Not mine. Though I could tell from the way she said it that she thinks her grandchildren are the smartest, bravest, cutest little people on planet Earth.

I wander into the kitchen on the lookout for bread and some sliced ham, maybe a bit of cheese, and the next thing you know I'm pulling flour and sugar out of the cabinet. Cans of peaches and pears, apples and cherries. Disposable tin-foil pans.

THE PHONE jars me out of a flour-dust stupor. I wipe dough on my apron—actually, Gloria's apron—and pull my cell out of my pocket.

"Jenny?"

"Rick?"

"Who did you think it would be?"

"I don't know. I don't read minds."

Rick's set mine fields in this conversation, and I just blew off one of my legs.

"What are you trying to pull, Jenny?"

"Nothing. I decided to stay in California."

"Without telling me?"

A second explosion, and there goes my right arm.

"I thought I'd surprise you."

"You certainly did."

From his tone of voice, I take it the surprise was a nasty one. Well, chalk one up to the new Jenny Miller, former pie-queen doormat.

"We could have discussed this, Jenny."

"I'm willing to discuss anything, anytime. Only not on the phone."

I look at the line of pies. If I eat them all I'll grow to the size of this house. Then I won't have to make any decisions at all except how to wedge myself into the shower.

"How do you expect me to discuss anything with you pouting out there on the west coast? I have a restaurant to run, Jenny. A daughter to take care of. Fires to put out."

"You sure know a lot about that, Rick. Putting out fires."

I just stepped squarely in a mine that knocked out my heart.

We listen to each other breathe a while, then we hang up. Me, first. I hope.

The pies sit there in accusing rows, and I can't tell you what I was seeking when I made them. Comfort in the familiar? Comfort in calories? Comfort in doing something I do well?

It would be a shame to waste all these pies. But I'm not fixing to take out a spoon. Instead, I get Gloria's car keys, make a shaky exit from the driveway, gain momentum two blocks down the street and zoom with confidence into the neighborhood Walgreen's. I purchase cellophane and ribbons, return home and tie the pies with pretty pink bows, then load them into the back of the Ferrari.

When the woman next door answers the bell, I say in my best perky voice, "Hello, you have just won a home-baked pie. Compliments of Jenny Miller."

"I didn't enter anything. How could I win?"

"Because you're a woman?"

She looks at me as if I've lost my last marble, then we both start laughing. I tell her I'm Gloria Hart's guest from Mississippi, and she invites me in for coffee.

Afterward, Ruth Clark, mother of two college-kids-driving-her-crazy, daughter of mother-in-a-nursing-home and wife of busy-lawyer-never-on-time-for-social-functions climbs into Gloria's fancy car and helps me deliver the rest of the pies to the unsuspecting public.

"I haven't had this much fun since my senior prom," she says, and I tell her I'm staying in California a while, perhaps we can be friends.

Sometimes you have to stop looking in order to find what you want.

—Gloria

IT'S TWO DAYS before Tuck and I come up for air enough to have a real conversation. And our first disagreement. Over a horse.

We're in his barn where he's introducing me to Moonchild and telling me I can ride, but only in the paddock with him leading the horse and holding the reins.

I ruffle up like a petticoat in a hundred-mile-an-hour wind.

"I won't be carried around on a silk pillow or

treated differently from any other woman around here."

"You *are* different."

"I most certainly am not."

"For me, you are. I'd die if anything happened to you."

Okay. Now I'm melting. Now I'm tempted to get on this horse and let him lead me around. But only for a moment. I didn't become who I am by letting anybody lead me around.

"I can take care of myself."

"I want to take care of you."

"Not by wrapping me in cotton batting, you won't."

"Would you be satisfied if I helped you into the saddle then rode along close by, just in case I need to catch you if you fall?"

"For how long?"

"What would you do if I said the rest of our lives?"

"I'd say you needed a different script writer. One who would include starlight and a great big moon and maybe a little harmonica music."

Tuck pulls a harmonica out of his pocket and

plays a blues riff. *See?* That's one thing I love: the surprise of this man.

"There's your music." He tucks it back in his pocket. "I think I can take care of the rest."

He's not kidding around, and neither am I. Falling in love is like being pregnant. You can't be just a little bit pregnant. You either are or you aren't.

You either fall in love or you don't. And it only takes an instant. Sure, it takes time to learn another person's habits, his quirks, his favorite music, his favorite foods. But if the chemistry is not there from the beginning, the grand passion will be missing, and what's the use without it?

"You don't even know what I eat for breakfast." I say this to test the waters.

"In the morning we'll get out of bed long enough to find out."

"And what about my TV show?" I'm looking for affirmation now, real commitment.

"I'm not afraid of flying."

With that he leads the horses outside, swings me into the saddle, mounts his huge black stallion, and we ride out side by side.

"See. I told you I can do this." Moonchild trots

down the lane at a sedate pace, and I feel as if I was born in the saddle.

Past the pasture gate, she speeds up and I wonder aloud why saddles don't come with handlebars.

"Have you ridden before?"

"Yes. But I never knew what they meant by *rolling gait*." The way I'm rolling, I could slide off any minute.

"How many times?"

"Once. On a segment of *Love in the Fast Lane*." The tree I'm passing teeters at an alarming angle, and when Tuck stops laughing, he reins in his stallion then helps me down.

"Are you always going to be this much trouble?"

"You can count on it."

Later that evening I learn about Tuck's favorite TV show—any channel that features sports. We're stretched out on his big leather sofa, my back against his chest, his legs wrapped securely around me, our hands clasped, fingers intertwined.

"You don't mind watching the game with me?"

I could tell you everything I know about ball—any kind of ball—in two words: practically nothing. Not because the games bore me, but I've lived mostly uninfluenced by the male persuasion.

People think I live this glamorous, full-to-the-brim life, and some envy me. They think I have it all. What they don't see is that the problems—from overflowed toilets to skylights leaking—are all mine.

They don't see the Thanksgivings spent eating take-out pizza for one. The Christmases when it seems useless to hang a stocking or put up a tree because who cares? The birthdays where the only surprise party I'm likely to get is the one I plan for myself then forget I've invited people over. The times I'm too sick to get out of bed and nobody's there to bring chicken soup. Even the dresses that zip in the back and I can only reach halfway up without assistance so I have to wear something else.

Some singles say nights are the worst, but that's not true. It's the evenings that are bad, those twilight hours after work and before bedtime when it's just you and the big empty house and you can no longer tell yourself you're busy and lucky and content. What you are is brutally, desperately lonely. And nobody is there to notice, let alone massage your temples and whisper, "Lean against me. Relax."

"Are you okay?" Tuck puts his big warm hands on my shoulders, massages them. "You seem tense."

I lean into him, feel myself letting go, just letting go. If this can be mine—the ease and peace and wonder of two like souls joined—then I am the luckiest woman in the world.

"I'm better than okay." I kiss his hands and the curved thumbs that are beautiful. "I love this. Just being here with you."

"Good. I'm glad."

Mort's call lures me away from my cozy nest, and I excuse myself and go into the kitchen.

"Claude wants to know when you're coming back to the show."

"Not when, Mort. If."

"He's made a tempting offer, Gloria." Mort talks money and I listen only half-heartedly. The daily grinds, the early morning makeup calls. Besides, how can I do daytime drama in Hollywood and have any kind of life in Mississippi? A few weekends here and there? Vacations and holidays?

"Give me a few days to make up my mind, Mort. Okay."

"Maybe this will help. You also have an offer from Jeff Shanks."

Academy Award-winning director. My agent certainly has my attention now.

"Tell me."

"It's an ensemble piece, a Southern drama similar to *Steel Magnolias* and *Crimes of the Heart*. You'd play the oldest of three sisters coming to grips with their traumatic past."

"Who are the other two actresses?"

"It's too early to say, but they're looking at a couple of box-office stars. You'd share billing. Also, the film has the advantage of moving you from the small screen into features."

The best advantage, though, is being on location a few weeks, perhaps a few months, then back home. And not leaving again until I find another role that interests me.

"What do you want me to tell Claude and Jeff, Gloria?"

"I still have some thinking to do, Mort. Okay?"

After I say goodbye, I stand in the kitchen and breathe. Simply breathe.

"Everything okay?" Tuck asks when I go back into the den, and I say "Yes," then slide into the best place in the world, the only place I want to be, cuddled against him enjoying the simple pleasure of being a woman in love with a special man.

We'll talk tomorrow. The real miracle is that we *have* tomorrow.

Who made me Oprah?

—Angie

DADDY'S looking at my scrapbook for the umpteenth time. Well, actually he's only looking at the parts that feature Mom. And I'll have to say she looks good in most of them, especially the ones Roberta took at the Magic Castle where Mom's all dressed up.

"Now, who did you say that was?"

"Roberta's brother-in-law." He's asked me this twice. He sounds just like Sally that time her cousin from Huntsville, Alabama, spent the summer in Mooreville and stole her boyfriend.

My gosh. My dad's *jealous*.

"Does he have a name?

"He's just some dorky guy, Dad. I don't remember his name. Forget about it."

"So." He clears his throat, which I absolutely

hate. That always means he's fixing to grill me. "Did she see him more than once?"

"For Pete's sake, Dad. It's not like Mom went out to California and started acting like she didn't have a wedding ring. Listen." I flip pages, turn past the ones where Mom's having such a good time at the pool party, which he would probably turn into a federal case for fornication, the way his mind's running.

"I want you to see the rally."

"I saw it."

"Yeah, but you didn't see how Mom was the one right up front. You didn't read the article about how she was the one who put the whole thing together."

Listen, I'm no dummy. I don't mind giving up my credit when it's for a good cause. And I can tell you right now, getting Mom back home is the best cause I know. Dad's been acting like a sick beagle puppy ever since I got home. Nearly three days. It's driving me crazy.

You ought to see him in the kitchen. He acts like he doesn't have a clue how to find stuff in the refrigerator, and him owner of a *restaurant*. He used to get the newspaper first thing every morning, and now I'll go out there at ten o'clock and it'll still be lying in the driveway.

He forgets things, like where he put his car keys and the hedge clippers and the *garden hose*, for Pete's sake. Who loses a garden hose? It's bigger than an alligator. Sometimes he even forgets to shave.

I'll be glad when school starts. I'll be glad when it's over and I'm officially eighteen and go live somewhere else without parents who are acting like eight-year-olds fighting over who gets the strawberry ice cream and who gets the chocolate.

Why don't they just get one dish and share?

And I don't want to even think about Jackson. He's been calling here every day, wanting to come over. I don't want to see him till Sally can help me figure out how not to break up when I tell him dating only one person is so totally out of the picture he can forget it.

I've made up umpteen excuses. I had to stay here and take care of dad. True. Kind of. I had to wash my hair. True. I had plans with Sally. A bald-faced lie. Though, of course, I *will* have plans with Sally, but not just yet, not till I can figure out how to keep Dad from unraveling.

He's worse than Mom. Listen, women know how to cry and get on with things. But men are a whole different story.

As far as I'm concerned, all this stiff-upper-lip, take-it-like-a-man stuff is for the birds. I want to say, *Listen, Dad, that went out with the Dark Ages. Men are enlightened now. They're not scared to have a sensitive side and let their feelings show.*

But what do I know? I'm only seventeen, right?

While I'm getting a pretty good handle on taking care of myself, there are just some problems I can't even understand, let alone fix.

Like this one. Dad's bent over my scrapbook like it's a patient and he's performing major life-or-death surgery.

"Are you sure she didn't see him again?"

Meaning Mom and the dork. Pardon me while I puke.

"Why don't you just fly out to California and see her?"

He shuts my scrapbook—well, *slams* is more like it—then stands there trying to look like somebody in charge. He'd die if I told him he was wearing one blue sock and one brown.

"I have a restaurant to run. Family obligations. Everybody seems to forget that."

"Jeez, Dad, I don't need a babysitter. I *am* a babysitter. And the last time I looked Mom was part of this family."

He just looks at me like I'm a specimen from Mars. Then he says, "The last time I looked you were six years old and crying about your first day at school."

His voice has gone all gruff and tender, the way it used to be when he'd come to tuck me in and read my favorite bedtime story—*The Velveteen Rabbit*.

"I'm all grown up, Dad."

"I see that now."

He hugs me, and I hold on tight, finally understanding the childhood story. When somebody loves you enough, you *do* become real.

Maybe that's why parents rock their babies and sing lullabies. Maybe that's why Mom is waiting in California.

And maybe I'll tell Dad. But not yet. I'd like for going after Mom to be his idea.

And I think she would, too.

CHAPTER 17

Does everybody have a god of second chances, and will I know mine if he comes?

—Jenny

I don't think I should have let Roberta, back from San Francisco and full of sass and vinegar, talk me into giving a dinner party just because she thought it would do me good. Now Max is standing in Gloria's front door with a bouquet of wilting daisies.

What would do me good is to slam the door in poor Max's face and run as fast as I can. Get out of this blue dress that shows off my newly tanned legs and act like a woman with no place to go and no idea of what she's going to do next. A woman who needs to sit down and make a few plans.

"Come in, Max," is what I say, and he marches in like a man who has a few plans of his own that might involve delivering more than flowers.

Did I also say that before I saw him I was thinking about that, too? A lot. A woman deprived will get all sorts of crazy ideas in her head, including whether the rest of Max is as wilted as his daisies.

Why doesn't Rick know this? And why is he sitting out there in Mooreville without so much as picking up the phone to ask if I'm okay? I haven't heard from him since Angie got home. A whole week ago.

"Can I get you something to drink? Coffee? Tea? Wine?"

Max says, "Wine," so I race off to the kitchen, grateful to have something to do. He's sitting on one end of the sofa looking hopeful, and I don't think I can deal with his expectations.

Instead I deliver the wine, then deliberately sit in a chair across the room.

"How are you, Max?"

"Fine. And you?"

"Great."

"That's nice."

"How was the drive over?"

"Good."

"Great."

Oh lord. I swig wine as if it's an artesian well and I've just emerged from the parched desert. Max crosses his right leg over his left, twists his mustache, then switches legs, left over right.

I dangle my shoe from the end of my foot and slug back wine, hoping for quick oblivion.

What's keeping Roberta and Hubert? Clearly Max and I aren't going to be an item. We can't even carry on a conversation. Things seemed different when we were in the Magic Castle, more hopeful, more exciting, more…I don't know…everything. Maybe that's the only place you can find magic, but I don't think so. I hope not.

When the doorbell rings, I hurry to the front door feeling rescued. Roberta will do all the talking, and I'll be off the hook. I can sit quietly and wait for the evening to end.

Putting on my biggest smile, I swing the door open saying, "At last!"

There stands my over-the-moon gorgeous husband. Still wearing his ring, thank goodness.

And smiling right back at me.

"How did you know I was coming? I wanted to surprise you."

"You did."

And, boy, do I have a surprise for him. My smile wobbles.

"But you're all dressed up." Rick peers behind me, then marches right in and spots Max, who would have been invisible if he'd just kept his seat. But *no*, he had to jump up like some besotted fool before I could think how to explain him.

"I see," Rick says.

What he sees is my poor hapless would-be suitor wearing a foolish grin and keeping a choke grip on the already beleaguered daisies. What I see is a big mess. The frozen tundra would be cozier than this room with this threesome.

Rick is sizing up Max with a look that forbodes annihilation. Which could include me.

"Here." I hurry over and pry the flowers out of Max's sweaty grip. "Let me put these in water."

It's called quitting the field of battle. Or cowardice. Whichever way you want to look at it.

I dawdle over finding the vase, let the water overrun the rim three times, then finally plop the poor gasping daisies in. I imagine them breathing a sigh of relief, saying to each other

Thank goodness, we thought we were going to have to call 9ll.

Maybe that's what I ought to do. Call right before the bloodletting so the stretcher is already handy.

"Jenny?"

Rick's in the doorway, and I jump as though I've been shot. Or am guilty. Which I am. Although I can't quit figure out why.

"Yes?" I try for perky and fail.

"If you think I'm leaving just because your lover is sitting there, you're mistaken."

"He's not my lover."

Rick just looks at the flowers and walks out of the kitchen. I wish I'd never put them in water. I wish I'd dumped them in the garbage can and that I'd been in the midst of the crime—killing poor innocent daisies—when Rick walked in.

I wish I'd thrown them into the sink, grabbed my husband and laid a great big smooch on him that would have made him forget the many small wounds we've inflicted on each other. I wish I could have made him forget everything except the relief of being back with me.

Oh, I excel at hindsight.

Of course, what would I have done if he'd forgiven the past? Gone back to being the same tired woman in the same stultifying routine?

The doorbell pings again—*oh, thank God!*—and I run to the door and cast myself on Roberta's mercy.

"Rick's here and he and Max are already in a pissing contest."

"Good. Bring on the wine." She breezes past, leaving poor Hubert to trail along in her wake. "So there you are," she yells at my husband. "Jenny's long-absent hunk."

She tugs Rick to the sofa where she plops down beside him and puts her hand on his knee. I don't see the rest because I've seen Rick's face, and that's enough. He looks exactly the way he does when Godzilla gets on his last nerve and he's getting ready to tell her to butt out of his business. Only not in those nice words.

Hiding once more in the kitchen, I dither over the wineglasses, the carafe, the tray. Even the placement of the pink mandevilla I brought into the house earlier and forgot to carry into the living room.

Then I remember that I chucked everything

that was familiar and secure and climbed into a Ferrari bound for Hollywood. And if all that was for nothing, I might as well have stayed home.

I should just climb in the garbage can, pull the daisies in behind me and tack an epitaph to the lid: Here lies Jenny, who never learned how to be a goddess but who made compounding mistakes into an art.

This could be my last chance to change my epitaph.

The woman who walks back into the den is not the same woman who scuttled out of it. Swishing my skirts, I priss right back in there and pass the wine with a steady hand and a firm smile, even though Rick's sizing me up.

You know how the back of your neck tingles when somebody you love is staring at you? How the hairs on your arms stand on end and you get goosebumps all over? Well, that's me, right this very minute.

And I think it's a good sign. It gives me courage to pull my chair close to Rick, put my hand on his knee and smile at him.

"I'm glad you came," I tell him, then I add, "honey," for good measure.

The rest of the evening is pleasant enough, with all of us making small talk, and Max even doing a few magic tricks, though nothing that involves me. Instead he pulls his scarves from Roberta's ears, his coins from Hubert's, his cards from his own seemingly bare hands.

I believe the reason we carry on like civilized adults is that one little word. *Honey*. Said as if I mean it.

Which I do.

After all the guests have gone, Rick and I go into the kitchen to clean up the last of the dishes. This is a familiar routine for us, one we do in comfortable silence. When the dishwasher is loaded, I untie Gloria's apron and move within touching distance of Rick.

"Did you bring your clothes?"

"They're in the car. But I booked a motel. Just in case."

"You don't need it." I wait for him to say something, anything, but he's the Sphinx and I'm a basket case. "Gloria has plenty of rooms."

The separate-bed issue drives us back to our corners, mine by the sink, Rick's by the table.

"Jenny? I'm sorry about overreacting earlier."

"I understand. I did the same thing about the pink note."

"Can we put it behind us?"

"I don't know, Rick. Can we?"

"I'd like to think so."

He still hasn't touched me. I'm standing here with my arms wrapped around myself, hoping he will. And hoping he won't. Not yet, at least. I want to get some things straightened out first.

If he so much as puts a hand on my cheek, I'm a goner. Rick's like a food allergy. You know your feet are going to swell and your arms will itch even before you take the first bite, but you take it anyway because the dish is so delicious you can't resist. That's me with Rick. Only the symptoms are different.

"What are we going to do?" I ask him.

"I'd like you to come home with me. I was hoping you would."

"It can't be the same. I can't go back to Mooreville and just start making pies."

"Why didn't you tell me you were tired of making pies?"

"It's more than that. I just got tired of everything."

Rick gets a bit ruffled at that, but I'll have to give him credit, he's trying hard not to show it, not to fall back into that old pattern where we always ended up in the same bed with our backs to each other, making sure our legs didn't touch.

"Look, Rick. I'm not blaming you."

"Does there have to be blame here, Jenny? I've had a few weeks to think about this."

Meaning, while he was home alone and I was in Hollywood flirting with a magician. But then, that's the kind of thinking that got me here in the first place.

"So have I, Rick. What I meant to say is, there are no good guys and bad guys in this relationship. We just sort of drifted away from each other and got lost in our separate routines." I pour myself a glass of water. Hand him one. "I guess most couples do."

"I guess."

He glances at the clock. It's the witching hour, when Cinderella loses her glass slipper and the coach turns into a pumpkin and deep conversations can turn productive or nasty, depending on how long you talk and who's the most persuasive and whose mood takes a nosedive.

"It's getting late."

Rick is always the one to point out the obvious. But he's also the one to see the hidden traps, the gopher holes just under the surface when I didn't even know we had gophers. So when he says, "We can talk about this in the morning," I simply say, "Okay."

He gets his clothes out of the rental car, then I show him the room down the hall.

"This was Angie's. She loved it." I'm bustling around, pointing out clean towels and the robe hanging on the bathroom door, turning down the sheets, keeping busy, trying to hide my flushed face and my disappointment.

I know. I know. I'm silly. Reason tells me we're doing the sensible thing, but my heart is a stubborn old fool. It wants violins and moonlight, mad embraces, sweaty bodies. Declarations.

Oh lord, most of all it wants *I love you*.

"The room's fine." He slips off his tie, tosses it on the bed.

"Well, goodnight, Rick."

"Goodnight, Jenny."

Later, lying in bed I think about his tie. Red with navy stripes. I gave it to him last Christmas.

"For special occasions," I told him because he hardly ever wears a tie. He hardly ever has a need. Weddings. Funerals. An occasional banquet where they honor the volunteer fireman of the year. He never even wears his tie on Sundays. We're casual in our little country church.

And yet...he wore it for me. I was his special occasion.

"Jenny?"

I didn't hear him come in, can barely see him in this ultra-dark room where the draperies are so thick and well-fitted hardly a sliver of moonlight seeps through. But I can smell him, the heady combination of sun and fresh air with just a touch of Old Spice.

I love that about Rick. That's he's not a Bulgari man. That in spite of his looks he has no conceits, no bloated ego.

I don't say anything, just pull back the covers and feel my husband slide in beside me. Without a word, we turn to each other, and I could swear to you the years fall away and we're once again the teenagers who fell in love and dreamed of living the rest of our lives together in the same beloved place where we grew up.

Afterward, when we hold each other close, I have that same dream. I hope Rick does, too.

Before I fall asleep, I promise myself we'll talk about it tomorrow. We'll talk about everything tomorrow.

CHAPTER 18

If you wake up in your own bed, was it all a dream?

—Jenny

When I wake up I'm disoriented and my head is pounding and I can't understand why pink light's pouring in when I distinctly remember closing Gloria's drapes.

Then I feel Rick's hand on my shoulder, hear him say "Jenny," and I know I'm not in California anymore; I'm in my own bed underneath the skylight which Rick has left open, as he always does when weather permits, so he can feel the first brush of dawn.

My head is pounding because Rick and I started a conversation on the west coast his first morning there that continued in the airplane and lasted a thousand miles.

"How are you?" he asks. More than anything it's Rick's anxiousness that makes me know I made the right decision.

We're both feeling our way. That's what his uncertainty says to me. *We both have some adjusting to do, some problems we need to work out, but my heart is tied up in the outcome, too.*

"Glad. That's how I am. Glad to be home, and excited, but a bit scared, too."

See. I'm learning to express myself. I'm learning not to end my sentences with a question even when they're not.

"Me, too."

Rick kisses me on the shoulder then sits up. When the sheet falls away, I see him as he was in high school. Perfect in every way.

But I see him as he is, too, the hairs on his chest going a bit gray, his muscles losing their tone, his hair a bit thinner. And he's still perfect in every way.

"What?" he says, the corners of his mouth turned up in a little half smile.

"I'm glad you're scared, and I'm glad you told me. I'm glad you're getting old, too, because I'd hate to be the only one."

"You're not the only one, Squirt."

I'm even glad to be called Squirt, because now I understand it's still a term of endearment, special because it's filled with a lifetime of shared memories.

"Let's go down to the restaurant," he says, and I nod, okay, then get out of bed and start putting on my clothes.

Angie's at Sally's, her last big all-night hoorah before school starts, so I don't have to worry that she'll wake up to an empty house. I'll see her later.

All she asked when we called to tell her we were coming home was, "How are you guys doing?"

"Fine," is what I told her yesterday, knowing that I'd talk to her when I got home. Really talk, because she deserves that. She's earned it.

Now, walking in the half-light holding hands, Rick and I go down the hill to his restaurant. Not through the woods as I did on my misguided midnight mission, but on the paved road, nothing to hide.

I've always viewed his restaurant as having a personality. It's Rick's home away from home, his taskmaster as well as his mistress, the other love of his life. Usually when I walk in, I'm intimidated. I feel as if I'm wearing the wrong shoes and the wrong color dress, the wrong hairdo, the wrong lipstick. I feel as if I'm in the boxing ring with a heavyweight championship contender, and I brace myself for the knockout punch.

Today, though, I see the restaurant as an empty building in need a face-lift. A good coat of paint on the walls going dull with smoke and grease. Something cheerful, like a bright sunny yellow. Some new curtains. A few jazzy new prints on the wall. Flowers from my garden on each table.

I tell all this to Rick, and he listens.

"We could take out that wall." I point, excited now. "Turn it into a room for our private parties."

He nods, approving.

The plan we started hatching in California and nursed all the way across the country is taking shape now.

I'll no longer be Jenny the pie maker, but Jenny the hostess, the woman who knows how to plan the best parties in Lee County. We'll do private bookings—Kiwanis club meetings, school and civic banquets, graduation parties, even wedding receptions.

Rick can trim back the restaurant's regular hours because expanded services will more than make up the lost income. The best part is that Rick and I will be together, working side by side to build our future.

But one thing we've learned. We'll play side by side, too. And we'll never, ever take each other for granted.

"I'll wear a costume," I tell him. "Something cute and perky with a short skirt that shows off my legs."

"You're kidding, right?"

I just wink at him then sashay toward his office while he hurries to catch up.

"Jenny? You *are* kidding, aren't you?"

I sit on the edge of his desk, hike up my skirt.

"Why don't you come on in here, big boy, and find out?"

When Rick walks in I say, "Lock the door," using my very best goddess voice.

Sometimes, suddenly, life makes sense and you no longer need a green-for-go emerald.

—Gloria

THE ROSES DELIVERED to my dressing room today are pink and the card says, Missing you, hurry home, although I've only been gone four days and will be back in Mooreville tomorrow.

And so will my Ferrari, I hope. Jackson flew to California with me and is driving it home. When I told him to take his time, enjoy the road trip, he said he was my slave for life. Tuck told him that role was already taken, he'd have to chose a lesser one.

If I keep thinking along these lines, I'll flub my story lines.

When I hear the knock on my door, I think it's my cue for *Love in the Fast Lane*, but it's Roberta, breezing in without waiting for me to say come in, wearing sunglasses with rhinestone frames although it's only eight o'clock in the morning and raining outside.

"This place looks like a flower shop." She goes from roses to violets to gardenias to birds-in-paradise, reading the cards. Every one of them private and every one of them from Tuck.

"He sends you flowers every day? That man's either lost his mind or he's horny as a horny toad."

"Good morning to you too, Roberta. What are you doing here besides reading my private mail?"

"What's private about a card stuck on a plastic stick in plain view? I came to talk about my retirement."

"You'll have to wait. My cue's coming up."

"That's not likely. Somebody forgot to bring Susan Star's pacifier and she's in her dressing room pitching a hissy fit."

"It's not her pacifier, it's me."

"She's jealous you're back, huh?"

"It seems that way. Even though she knows this is a guest shot and I'll only be here once in a blue moon."

"That's enough to steal her thunder. If you ask me, she never had any in the first place. That old fox was a fool to lose you at sea."

There's a knock on my door. "Miss Hart. Ready for you on the set."

I grin at Roberta. "Well, he's found me now, and my island paradise awaits."

I used to think Jillian Rockwell was the best part of me. But as I enter the hot glare of stage lights I realize that the best part of me is curled inside, waiting to get back to the farm where I can unfold, spread my wings, ride a horse, read in a hammock, hang on to the paddock fence watching Tuck transforming another horse into a champion.

Still, I enjoy the excitement of being on a set, making a story come to life for loyal fans who never stopped believing in me, who fought for me. And won.

So I give them Jillian, rediscovered on her exotic island where she is determined to live the rest of her days in peace.

Oh, I know the writers. They'll throw in a few good works and a bit of drama. An old priest whose church Jillian saves. An island child suffering from a rare disease that only Jillian's money and influence can cure. Maybe even a romantic interest who looks a lot like Tuck.

And that's fine with me, because I control the number and frequency of guest shots.

After I leave the set and get out of my stage makeup, I take Roberta to her favorite Mexican restaurant for lunch.

"Now, let's talk about retirement," I say.

"If you think I'm going to abandon you and go off on some prolonged trip cooped up in a camper listening to Hubert snore, you've lost your tiny mind. I just figured we'd talk about how I could handle things out here since you'll be getting married and living in Mooreville."

"Who said anything about marriage?"

"That ruby ring on your left finger."

Red for stop. Red for passion. Red for love. Tuck gave it to me last week after I told him about the emerald.

"You can stop now, Gloria," is what he told me. "Right here in Mooreville. Just stop and rest."

What he meant by that was *just stop and be*, in the very best Zen-like sense.

"Roberta, you've been watching too many segments of *Love in the Fast Lane*."

"You're not going to marry that man? Well, step aside, honey. Let me at him."

"Perhaps. Eventually. But right now we're just enjoying being together."

Of course, *enjoy* is too mild for what we have, but Roberta's smart enough to read between the lines.

She's also smart enough to know that I'll need someone to carry on out here as long as I decide to keep my career. So over chimechangas, we work out the details.

Then I tell her about the role I've accepted in the Jeff Shanks movie.

"I guess we'd better be working on adding some good nursing-home coverage to my health care plan."

"Why?"

"At the rate you're going, starting a whole 'nother career at your age, I'll be needing assisted living by the time you're accepting your Academy Award." Roberta calls for a refill on her margarita. "Now tell me about them Miller girls."

"Those. And I thought you'd given up bad grammar."

"I just wanted to keep you on your toes."

"Why don't you come to Mooreville to see for yourself?"

I pull two tickets out of my purse and hand them to her. It's the only time I've ever seen Roberta cry, which tells me Hubert kept my secret in spite of his awe of Roberta.

MY FERRARI arrived in Mooreville, and so did fall. Just in time for the grand reopening of Rick's restaurant.

We all pile in to the car—Roberta and Hubert, who are our guests at the farm, Tuck and I—then head to the restaurant where Jenny and Rick, arm in arm, are greeting guests in the doorway. Backlit by the lights pouring from the main dining room Jenny told me they've repainted a color called daffodil, they look like a Hallmark painting for an anniversary card.

This is the way I imagined Rick and Jenny when I first came to Mooreville, before I learned that looks can deceive, relationships can change and the road back home can sometimes be an arduous journey.

"Everybody in Mooreville saw Jillian's return to the show," is the way Jenny greets me. "We hooked up a big-screen TV in the main dining room so we wouldn't miss it. Come inside. I can't wait for you to see what we've done."

She sweeps Roberta into her embrace and drags her along, too. For a moment our fierce band of female warriors holds its tight circle in the middle of the room, but I get waylaid by Elaine and Lanford wanting the inside scoop on *Love in the Fast Lane*, while Jenny gets pulled away by Patty Jones wanting to ferret out the latest gossip.

I glance back at Roberta, who gives me a

thumbs-up, and I know that no matter how many directions we go, the three of us will still be together, bound by loyalty, laughter and the war wounds of living, cemented by hearts and souls and spirits that never give up. No matter what.

Jenny escapes her nosey neighbor's clutches and takes the microphone set up on a newly erected small stage at the back of the restaurant.

"Welcome to our grand reopening. We have food and drinks for everybody, but first I'd like to call a very special person to the stage. Angie, will you come up here?"

Angie joins her mother, black lipstick replaced by pink, big attitude tamed but not broken as she slides her arm around her mother's waist.

"Though Angie's eighteenth birthday was last week, we wanted to share the celebration with all of you."

Rick wheels out an enormous cake, somebody starts singing "Happy Birthday," and suddenly there's confetti everywhere.

My gift for Angie is tucked in my pocket, wrapped in festive paper and tied with a pink bow. My green-for-go emerald. Angie needs it now. She's growing up, moving up, moving on.

She has the kind of energy and drive I had at eighteen. I don't know her plans, and I don't think she does either, but I've no doubt she'll find her way.

Tuck comes up behind me, kisses my neck, brushes confetti out of my hair.

"Hey, you. Penny for your thoughts."

"I was just thinking I've died and gone to Mooreville, Mississippi."

"It can be a paradise. If you don't count the mosquitoes and hundred-degree summer days and the humidity that makes it hard to breathe. And if you don't count the Patty Joneses and Lanfords and Elaines who want to know every bit of your business and aren't shy about telling it. And if you don't count the days I'll be too dog-tired even to take off my boots."

"Are you trying to scare me off?"

"Just stating the facts so you'll know what's in store for you."

"I know. And who's counting?"

We link arms and merge with the crowd.

Since I wrecked my car because of a cow, I've learned that there's more than one way to count, and the best is counting blessings.

Okay, so it *was* a big spotted dog and not a cow, but what can I say? Since I've given up constant TV stardom in favor of real life, I've become a real goddess.

And goddesses know that life is more fun with a bit of pizzazz, a dash of smoke and mirrors, a few fast friends and a whole lot of love.

* * * * *

Be sure to return to NEXT in December for more entertaining women's fiction about the next passion in a woman's life. For a sneak preview of Susan Crosby's novella, "YOU'RE ALL I WANT FOR CHRISTMAS," *which is part of the* THREE WISE WOMEN *holiday anthology, coming to* NEXT *in December, please turn the page.*

CHAPTER 1

Sun, sand and margaritas...*that* was Lauren Wright's plan, her Christmas gift to herself. Instead, three days before Christmas, she'd gotten *this*—Chicago's O'Hare airport during the worst weather delays of the year.

Lauren glanced around the gate area, her home away from home for the past two hours. Her gaze settled briefly on a man, one worthy of the second, third and tenth looks she'd given him. Mid-forties, she guessed, like her. Rugged, in a lumber-jack sort of way. He wore jeans, a forest-green shirt and an aged brown leather jacket. Add to that his wavy chestnut hair, olive skin and eyes so blue she could see the brilliant color from twenty feet away, and he was one tempting package.

No sooner did the woman sitting beside her leave than someone took her seat. A man. *The* man.

"I have a proposition for you," he said.

His eyes sparkled. His teeth flashed white. He smelled good. Really good. Like pine trees after a rainstorm.

Then his words registered. "A proposition?"

"I'll buy you a cup of coffee, if you'll save me this seat."

She felt her face heat up a little, her imagination having spun other much more interesting propositions. "I'd be happy to."

"Great, thanks. I'm Joe, by the way."

"Lauren."

"What would you like?"

You. Whoa. Where had that come from? "Um. A decaf mocha would be good. No whipped cream."

He dropped his bag onto the chair and walked away, giving her the opportunity to really look at him—tall, sturdy, outdoorsy. Great butt.

And no wedding ring.

Out of the corner of her eye, she tracked Joe's return. She wished she'd kept her book out so that she could look occupied, but she'd given up on it an hour ago, since there was plenty to hold her attention in the overcrowded terminal—especially the man walking toward her, a mini-fantasy come to life.

He passed her the coffee then took the seat.

"Thanks," she said, lifting the cardboard cup in a quick toast.

"My pleasure."

He nodded toward a kid who'd tossed his gear on the floor and crashed, falling asleep instantly and soundly. "So, what do you think his story is?"

"His story?"

"Where's he headed, do you suppose? Home from college for Christmas? Some happy mom waiting at the airport for him?"

She considered the young man, envying his ability to tune out the world and sleep in public. "A freshman." She cocked her head, considering. "Maybe not seeing his mom, yet. Maybe he's joining his father first to go skiing over Christmas, so now he's headed to Aspen to hook up with Dad and his new wife. Then he'll go home to spend the rest of his break with his mother—as much as a kid that age stays home," she added, smiling, remembering her first Christmas home as a freshman. She felt Joe's steady and sympathetic gaze on her, as if he knew it wasn't a story she was making up. "Just a guess," she added.

"First Christmas without your son?" Joe asked.

She nodded then sipped her mocha rather than add anything that might show how hurt she'd been by her son's choice. Jeremy could've gone skiing at New Year's instead, but he hadn't. Instead he'd chosen to leave her alone on Christmas—the worst day of the year.

Which was why she'd planned a getaway herself.

"Pretty ticked off at your ex for stealing him away?" Joe asked.

Had he been there and done that? "How'd you guess?"

He touched her hand for a second, the one holding—squeezing—the coffee cup. "I'm surprised you didn't pop the lid off."

Lauren went utterly still at the electrifying contact. The simple touch had zapped her clear down to her toes. Her eyes met his. She'd thought he'd sat beside her only so that he wouldn't lose a seat permanently, but maybe he'd been checking her out, too?

She decided to enjoy the flight delay as an adventure, and let herself be flattered by the way she occasionally caught him checking her out, and how content he seemed being near her. What could it hurt, after all? Ships passing in the night, that was all.

COMING NEXT MONTH

#97 THREE WISE WOMEN: A Christmas Anthology • Donna Birdsell, Lisa Childs and Susan Crosby

Here are three unforgettable stories of women drowning in all the glad tidings, good cheer—and stress!—of the season. And even if a tall, dark stranger doesn't top their Christmas lists, it may be just what Santa ordered…so watch as these women wise up to love in the holidays!

#98 ANNIE ON THE LAM: A CHRISTMAS CAPER • Jennifer Archer

When the bloom goes off the magnolia, Southern heiress Annie Macy comes to New York for a new lease on life—and runs smack-dab into her new boss's money-laundering scheme. Filching the files that prove his guilt during the office Christmas party lands her in hot water, until handsome P.I. Joe Brady leads Annie to safety…by way of the mistletoe.